Cast Iron Stake Through the Heart

Val,

Thanks so much for helping w/ this book!
I always need other sets of eyes looking for all my mistakes!

love,
Jodi

Val,

This was so much fun to work with Jodi on! Thanks for beta reading!

-♡- rebecca grubl

Cast Iron Stake
Through the Heart

Book 4 in The Cast Iron Skillet Mystery Series

Jodi Rath and Rebecca Grubb

Leavensport, Ohio

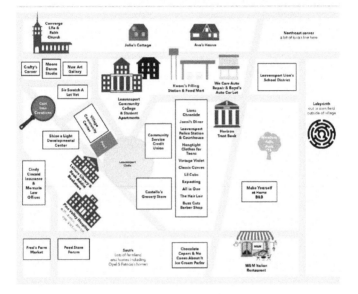

Converge Life & Faith Church

Julie's Cottage

Ava's House

Northeast corner
a lot of Joan's live here

Crafty's Corner

Moore Dance Studio

Nuu Art Gallery

Sir Scratch A Lot Vet

Cast Iron Creations

Village Community Center

Shine a Light Developmental Center

Leavensport Community College & Student Apartments

Kwan's Filling Station & Food Mart

We Care Auto Repair & Boyd's Auto Car Lot

Leavensport Lion's School District

Lions Chronicle

Jenni's Diner

Leavensport Police Station & Courthouse

Hangtight Clothes For Teens

Vintage Violet

Classic Curves

Lil Cubs

Expecting

All in One

The Hair Lair

Buzz Cuts Barber Shop

Horizon Trust Bank

Labyrinth
out in corn field
outside of village

Community Service Credit Union

Leavensport Cafe

Cindy Cincaid Insurance & Mercurio Law Offices

Castello's Grocery Store

Make Yourself at Home B&B

Fred's Farm Market

Feed Store Forum

South
Lots of farmland
and homes including
Opal & Patricia's homes

Chocolate Capers & No Cones About It
Ice Cream Parlor

M&M Italian Restaurant

It's best if you throw your personal baggage over a cliff, except then you'd have to go with it.

–Jodi Rath

Dedications

Writing is more of a labor of love than what I could have ever imagined. As an avid reader since grade school, I assumed writing would be an easy task. I mean, I love to analyze as well, so between all the reading and analysis I've done, writing a book should be a piece of cake, right? WRONG!

This dedication is to writers that have come before me and those out there doing the REAL-DEAL writing. The writers who are sacrificing their time and lives to put a great crafted story together for others' enjoyment. It is a true labor of love. Sara Paretsky, Agatha Christie, Flannery O'Connor, Emily Dickinson, Donna Leon, Patricia Cornwell, Mary Shelley, Laura Childs, Bailey Cates, Margaret Atwood, and Sheila Connolly (Rest in Peace) among SO many more wonderful writers. Thank you to all the writers who have inspired me over the years to take on such a laborious profession (mentally, spiritually, and yes—believe it or not, physically). Reading a book is one thing, writing is something *completely* different that no one understands unless they have done it.

It's important to take a moment to thank the educators that have changed my life. Mrs. Pumphrey was my Kindergarten teacher who was always so kind and caring and fun. She was a motherly figure which was so perfect to have when starting something new. Mr. Weaver who taught middle school English and made us understand how to effectively communicate with each other through reading and writing. My sophomore reading teacher Mr. Pierce, who is the reason I wanted to be a high school English teacher. He was a writer too. He created every single one of his grammar tests and added so much humor to the test—it was the only class I've ever taken where multiple students would burst into laughter while taking his tests. Only he could make students excited for test day on grammar! Dr. Yuckman was my college Shakespearean professor. He never gave me an A and I was an English Literature major. I took three of his courses because I was determined to get that A. That never happened, but I did learn SO much about where writing started, figurative language, themes and their importance in any piece of writing, and about true embarrassment when I pronounced "Thames" the way it is spelled in front of the entire class and he corrected me—LOL!

Then, thanks to my family and my team of women who help me put these books together—from covers to formatting to editing to the beta readers who double-check it all when we *think* we are done.

It's a real process that has taken me an entire lifetime to figure out. Heck, I'm still figuring it out as I go. But the ride has been amazing and I have no plans to stop—if I can keep writing after death, then sign me up!

–*Jodi Rath*

The first name in this dedication has to be Jodi Rath, who believed in my writing skills enough to trust me with half of a book in a series that she spent years creating and breathing life into. Writing this book has been an adventure, but all along the path, Jodi has been there, holding my hand, giving me advice, and sending me sassy emails to make me laugh. I thank her for this opportunity. It has been so fun!

Next, I dedicate (my half) of this book to my family, who has always supported my writing aspirations. This book wouldn't be possible without all of the times my husband put the kids to bed and did the dishes so I could write. Thanks to my parents, who provided me with a childhood full of reading. I also want to thank my twin sister, Susanna, who has been poking me to write since we shared a womb.

I don't have space to thank every author I have read, but they have all contributed to this book through me: Douglas Adams, Sir Arthur Conan Doyle, Toni Morrison, Yvonne Vera, Thomas Hardy, Charlotte Bronte, Annie Proulx, Gillian Flynn, and Lauren Goff.

Finally, I dedicate this book to all of my English teachers, particularly Stephanie Kight, whose class introduced me to so many amazing books. Thank you!

–Rebecca Grubb

The Leavensport Crew

Jolie Tucker—Co-owner of Cast Iron Creations, born in the village, best friend of Ava, granddaughter of Opal, daughter of Patty.

Ava Martinez—Co-owner of Cast Iron Creations, born in the village, best friend of Jolie, girlfriend of Delilah, sister of Lolly, daughter of Sophia and Thiago.

Keith—Ex-boyfriend of Jolie, born in the village, best friend of Teddy—now, an officer of Leavensport.

Detective Mick Meiser—Love interest of Jolie, from Tri-City, transferred career to Leavensport.

Chief Teddy Tobias—Police chief of Leavensport and born in the village, best friend of Keith.

Lydia—Jolie's frenemy, dating Bradley (or is she?) village nurse, best friend of Betsy, born in the village.

Betsy—Owns Chocolate Capers, best friend of Lydia, born in the village.

Delilah—Sister of Bradley, village artist, girlfriend of Ava.

Bradley—Brother of Delilah, village journalist, dating Lydia—maybe.

Grandma Opal—Jolie's grandma, housewife who helped Jolie and Ava start Cast Iron Creations with her cast-iron skillet recipes.

Aunt Fern—Jolie's wacky, unpredictable aunt, sister to Patty, man-hungry.

Patty—Jolie's mom.

Jackson Nestle—Unscrupulous political associate of Mayor Cardinal from Tri-City

Tink—Jolie's cousin that she only recently realized she had.

Tom Costello—Grocer in Leavensport; dating Grandma Opal

Niko Mercurio—Leavensport lawyer

Quinn Kingsley—Leader of art commune

Tad—Acting major, boyfriend of Alyssa

Darla Frederickson—Acting major

Mod—No major, abstract painter

Alyssa—Graphic design major

Lahiri—Liberal arts major

Poppy—Special effects major

Allison—Painter, lives in Painter's House

Linzie—Painter, lives in Painter's House

Chapter One

"Happy birthday to you! Happy birthday to you! Happy birthday, dear Jolie! Happy birthday to you!" My family, friends, and many village residents sang out to me in the community center. I fake smiled through it. I absolutely hated being the center of attention. Everyone who knows me understands this—but it doesn't stop my family from insisting on these events annually.

Twenty-five. The first part of my twenties was pretty rocky as I began dealing with issues from my past. Who am I kidding? I'm still working through things, and will be for some time–but at least I can see a light at the end of the tunnel now. That is something I did not have before. And light in the darkness is a good thing! I'm determined to turn my life around this year.

Speaking of lights, time to blow out all twenty-five candles. Not an issue for me.

One of my close friends, Betsy, runs a bakery in town called Chocolate Capers. For my birthday she made my absolute favorite cake, a Love at First Sight Triple Chocolate Crunch Cake. The title enough was a mouthful, but the cake . . . good Lord, the cake.

Betsy used her homemade chocolate icing, and because she knew how much I loved chocolate, she made it with double the amount of cocoa the recipe called for. I could eat the icing alone.

The cake itself was a moist, three-layer cake with that homemade frosting between each layer. The "crunch" in the name was from tiny bits of toffee throughout. I'd never tasted anything like it before. The only problem was I didn't want to share it with anyone. An only-child thing, probably. I hated to share.

"Psst, Jolie," Betsy nudged me to get my attention.

"Thanks so much for making this cake for me, Betsy! I know you don't make it often because it's a labor of love—making three for the party had to take a lot of time on your part," I grabbed her and gave her a big bear hug.

"This is true. But I wanted to tell you that these are for all of us. There is one in a cake container in the back just for you." Her hazel eyes sparkled as she smiled, her freckles dancing on her cheeks.

She knows me too well.

"What are you two whispering about?" Ava interrupted.

"Nothing," I said and then quickly changed the subject. "Hey, did you tell Betsy how you are such a renaissance woman now?"

"What are you talking about?" Ava put hands on hips, shifting to one side.

"What? You co-own our restaurant, you're now an officially licensed PI, *and* we're starting a side hustle of online cooking courses for people who want to learn to cook with cast iron," I said.

"Whoa, Ava, that's a lot! Are you getting bored with your life or something?"

"Anything but! We fell into helping to solve crimes. So, after solving the second crime in less than six months, I figured I might as well make some money off of it. I mean, we are pretty good at it. Then, when we were in Santo Domingo in February, Jolie and I saw an online cooking class for Dominican food. We discussed this as an option for us to expand and grow our business."

"Wow, you two are true entrepreneurs," Betsy said.

"Hey, if it works out well, maybe you can take a cut and do an entire class on baking," I said.

"I would love that. And Jolie, you could work with me so that we keep your and Ava's theme of baking in cast iron."

"Perfect!" Ava and I said in unison.

"Hey, I've got a mystery for you to solve." Delilah had sauntered up to us.

"What?" Ava looked alarmed.

"What the heck is up with Jolie's Aunt Fern?" She pointed through the crowd to where Aunt Fern stood with her hands on her hips, gazing into the crowd intently for a few seconds, then swiveling her head and looking in a different direction for a few seconds. She resembled a hawk searching for prey.

"There is a very real part of me that doesn't actually *want* to know ..." I began, but Betsy, Delilah, and Ava were already crossing the room, pulling me with them.

"Aunt Fern!" Ava hooted with her usual goofy, energetic flattery that kept her on my family's good side way more often than I was. "You always look gorgeous, but today you could win a beauty pageant. What gives?"

"Oh, Ava, you sweet girl," Aunt Fern giggled, patting her hair. "I'll tell you what gives. I got flowers on my doorstep this morning! And do you know what the card said? 'From your secret admirer'! So now I'm looking around, trying to figure out who that might be." She resumed staring around the crowd.

"Well, whoever it is would be lucky to have you," offered Delilah, but Aunt Fern seemed to have stopped listening. Betsy, Delilah, Ava, and I wandered back to our spot.

"The Case of Aunt Fern's Incognito Admirer," I intoned.

Betsy giggled. "Hey, you two should take on the case of the digging in the fields for sale beside M&M's Italian Restaurant."

"Is that still happening?" I asked. I thought back to a few months ago when Ava and I were headed for the airport to the Dominican Republic in the middle of the night, and I thought I had seen someone digging in the fields at two in the morning. Turned out to not be a figment of my imagination.

"Yep, Teddy has been adding more police presence around the area, but no one has seen anyone doing anything," Betsy said.

"Are you and Teddy getting any closer?" I asked, wondering where things stood with them.

Betsy's hazel eyes showed a speck of pain as she looked to the ground, "Um, no, we are just friends. I think he and Tabitha are dating."

"I'm sorry I brought it up." I cringed and sent a

sidelong glance to Ava.

"Betsy, that cake was absolutely delicious!" Ava saved me while giving me an out.

Betsy touched Ava's arm warmly, smiled, and moved back into the crowd.

I took that as my opportunity to take off. "I'm going to head home. We have a big day tomorrow with running the restaurant, finishing up our planning for our first class, then the big night where we start our online course!"

"Wait, this is your birthday party. You can't leave!" Ava declared.

"I've been hiding out in the kitchen for most of it. I ate and we did the cake. Everyone is having a nice time. No one will notice." I grabbed my tote and headed back to the kitchen to duck out the back door.

As I turned, I caught Ava grinning and rolling her eyes at me. She knew I always preferred being alone, and I hated large crowds. They made me nervous. My family knew this as well, but it never stopped them from expecting me to do holidays and doing things like setting up birthday parties with lots of people.

I double checked that I had turned everything off in the kitchen, since I had done most of the cooking for my own party, and that I'd cleaned up as much as possible then headed out back to get in my car and head home to cats, pajamas, TV, a book, and my cozy couch.

Opening the car door and shoving the heavy tote across the driver side to the passenger seat, I was startled when someone tapped my shoulder.

I turned and gasped, I couldn't believe it, "Hey, Mick."

Mick Meiser and I had a bit of a history, an off-and-on relationship that, as of last holiday season, was *off*. Ava and I had left the month of February and Mick and I had stayed in contact from video calls, and texting. We made an agreement we would sit down alone and talk through everything when I returned.

"Long time no see." He glanced off to the side uncomfortably.

Yeah, that was a problem. When I got back to Leavensport in March, I saw Mick taking Lydia, my life-long frenemy, into the OBGYN. I knew she was pregnant but didn't know who the father was. Next thing I knew, Meiser was gone. Supposedly, he had some undercover work to do in an "unknown" place. He had taken his two cats Stewart and the cat Lucky I brought back from Santo Domingo. He had not bothered to let me know he was leaving.

"I'm not a fan of the scruff," I said, noting his five o'clock shadow. I also noticed he wasn't using his cane anymore.

Meiser laughed and rubbed his chin. "Yeah, me neither. I had to do it for the case. Sorry I didn't reach out. I wasn't allowed to."

"So, this is something that came up from Teddy or from Tri-City? Does it have something to do with the digging in the fields by your restaurant?" I asked. Meiser worked at Tri-City first, then came to Leavensport to help Chief Teddy Tobias out. It was supposed to be temporary, but he ended up staying on in Leavensport, only doing side work now and then in Tri-City as needed.

"The city. I really can't get into it, Jolie. So, how are you feeling about everything?"

I shrugged my shoulders. "It's been a while. In

some ways, it feels like a lot has happened, and in other ways, it feels like not much has changed. Do you know what I mean?"

"Yeah, I get it. Life goes on. Time changes us." He looked at me with his big brown eyes. What was so disturbing was that this time, I didn't feel what I used to feel.

"You said it," I said, pulling my keys out of my pocket. "Well, I have to get going."

"Okay, see you around." Meiser began walking away.

I sat in my car and got ready to close the car door when he said, "Oh, and Jolie—"

I looked at him.

"Happy birthday."

I was snuggled up on my couch in my black "heart of courage" nightgown. I bought it after a breast cancer marathon I attempted to run but ended up having to walk. My four cats were splayed out on the blanket, draping across my feet and legs. Bobbi Jo was curled up on my belly as I held the TV remote in one hand, a glass of red wine in the other, and a half-eaten piece of Betsy's delectable cake sat on the coffee table. I was stuffed, but I kept eyeballing the rest of that piece sitting there begging for me to finish it. I began to shift, trying to pull my body out from my cat blanket to reach for the cake when the doorbell rang.

"Who is it?" I bellowed from the couch, annoyed someone was bothering me. I mean, it is my birthday and I'd seen everyone this afternoon. You'd think if someone wanted to be alone on their birthday they should be allowed.

"It's me! Ava!"

Why on earth was she knocking? Something must be wrong.

"You have a key. USE IT!" I yelled. I hadn't wanted to disturb the cats by getting up, but my screaming caused two of the four to jump down anyway.

"Geesh, someone is grumpy about aging." Ava trotted in and locked the door behind her.

Leavensport, Ohio had always been a safe place to live where everyone knew everyone else's business and most of us grew up here. Most of our elders knew us since birth and reminded us of that if and when we ever got out of line.

The last year had proven that times were definitely changing with more crime popping up. There was a time I left my door unlocked and my garage door open while at home. Those times were long gone since I'd had two break-ins within one month's time. Not to mention all of the other trouble Ava and I had gotten ourselves into lately.

"Why are you knocking?" I asked, sitting up and reaching for the cake.

"Hey, you bailed out before everyone else and when I left there was no cake. I was going to bring some home."

"Aw, you were thinking of me?" This was so unlike Ava.

"Not you, idiot! I wanted some leftovers! She never makes that cake."

Figures.

"I snuck a piece before I left," I said taking a big bite. I might have been willing to share except for that last comment.

"Well, that's a big piece. I'm going to go grab a—what!? Jolie Lynn Tucker, you LIAR!"

Ava must have seen the entire cake on my island in the kitchen.

"What?"

"A piece? She made you an entire cake! No wonder you were so gung-ho to get out of there this afternoon. I can't believe you don't have more of it gone."

I walked into the kitchen in time to see Ava take a huge slab that equaled three pieces.

"What are you doing?"

"I'm gonna eat a little now and take a little home since you are such a fibber."

"I was willing to share until you said you weren't going to bring me any home!"

Ava took a huge bite and her big mocha eyes lit up. I could tell all was forgiven so I went and grabbed what I had left as well.

"So, again, why did you knock? What's wrong?"

"Why do you assume the worst always?"

"You never knock. There's something you don't want to tell me," I said, knowing my bestie too well.

"I debated telling you today or waiting. I hate giving you bad news on your birthday, but I feel it's better you hear it from me."

I put my fork down, pushed the cake away, and looked at Ava with the give-it-to-me-straight look.

"Okay, here goes. After you left this afternoon, Bradley and Lydia had a showdown at the party. He demanded to know who the father of that baby is."

"He told me it wasn't his. He seemed sure. This was back when we were in Santo Domingo." I recalled my phone conversation with him. I had been trying to pry the information from him to be sure it wasn't Meiser's baby.

"Well, it looks like there are three possibilities and all three names came out in front of everyone. It was a huge scene. You missed it."

"Who are the three candidates?"

"Turns out Bradley is one of the three. Lydia said Keith was another possibility. And the last—" Ava looked off unable to meet my eyes.

My heart fell.

"Mick," I whispered.

"That's what she said. Then, she faked a cramp like a little coward and ran off."

"And everyone heard?" I asked.

"They were yelling to the point everyone was quiet and watching. So, yeah, they all heard. But I don't think everyone from the village was there."

"That doesn't matter at all. You know as well as I do it spread from house to house within minutes."

"Well, no one seems to know anything for sure."

"Was Mick there when the fight happened? What was his reaction?" Oddly enough, this afternoon when he and I spoke, I didn't feel that tingle I always felt around him and thought maybe I was moving on. But Ava coming in and laying all this in my lap had my heart and mind racing.

"I saw him sprint out the door when you left. He must have been watching you. I figured he was running after you as usual."

"Yeah, we talked briefly."

"You two finally settle anything?"

"What do you think? Oh man, what about my family?" I took a gulp of my wine and swallowed down the wrong pipe and began to choke on wine and cake.

"Oh yeah, they heard. I had to hold Grandma Opal back. I thought she was going to attack Lydia. Your mom just wanted to know where you were and for once, she was happy you left early."

I checked my cell, "I have no texts, no emails, no voicemail, and no one has beat down my door?"

"You're welcome. I had a little convo with the entire Tucker clan letting them know I'd handle this one. I said I'd come straight here and talk to you. I reminded them of all the work you've been putting into yourself with journaling and therapy and that it would go a *long* way for you forgiving them for holding out on you about your uncle and cousins if they were to allow you to come to them with this."

Ava was referring to last Thanksgiving's dysfunctional Tucker family disaster when I found out I had a long-lost uncle, aunt, and five cousins that no one ever bothered to tell me about. All because of some supposed squabble. They had all been living in Tri-City my whole life—thirty minutes away.

Wow, I wanted to grab Ava's cheeks and give her a huge smooch. "You are truly the best friend a gal could ever ask for!"

"Absofreakinglutely I am!"

We both laughed.

The next day Ava and I had called some of the staffers in to cover for us for the afternoon so we could prepare for our first online course that evening. One of us would normally be there from open until late afternoon, and we took turns closing. Recently, however, we were able to give Carlos, our longtime chef, a raise and promotion to assistant manager. Adding him to the mix gave us more flexibility to pursue other projects.

It was a great opportunity for Carlos as well, and he had certainly earned it. He had been a complete life-saver when Ava and I had to leave for almost a month. Some of Ava's family issues took us to the Dominican Republic in February, and Carlos kept the restaurant afloat. He even came up with some wonderful new cast iron Mexican cuisine and made those dishes the daily specials that week. Our sales skyrocketed since there wasn't a Mexican restaurant in our village—the closest was thirty miles away. When we saw the increase of sales, rewarding Carlos was a no-brainer.

"So, we decided we're calling our online class 'Cooking with Cast Iron,' correct?" Ava asked.

"Um, yeah, we put that on the syllabus we sent out and used it on all the email subject lines," I said this with a DUH tone.

"You were the one who took care of all that and the registration, so I wasn't sure." Ava cocked her head, glaring.

"Yes, that's the name." I changed my tone to add a hint of sunshine. Ava was the one who ran the front of our business. She took care of most of the paperwork and finances and did a great job. Once she learned a software program and created a routine, she was like a machine. The learning curve for new technology was always a challenge, though. Before we even started setting up, I was anticipating a lot of eye rolls and clenched shoulders. I knew by the time class started, my body would be twisted up in knots like a pretzel.

"No, just let me figure out how to log us in. You have to stand in a certain place. I have a cord with a camera attached to the computer. Bradley is going to be here to follow us with the camera, Ava. You don't need to shove your face into the computer screen each time you speak, and you don't have to shout, they'll be able to hear you."

This is *exactly* what I knew was coming this afternoon.

"Okay, Geesh, calm down! We gave this group a deep discount as a test group since we are new to all this. So, if we mess anything up, we don't have to feel bad about it!"

"I know. I just want to come off as professional."

"Because you have perfectionist Type-A issues."

"You've known me since I was born and you're my best friend, so you can't really diss me." I crossed my arms.

"It's annoying sometimes."

Oh, okay, *I'm* annoying. I'm not the one sticking my face in the camera and screaming—but I'll keep that as internal monologue because we need to move on.

"Bradley just pulled into my drive. You go meet him and help him bring whatever he has in—he's a tech genius too, so if we do have something mess up, he can help us. I will work on getting all the kitchen pans, gadgets, and food out and ready to go and figure out what we can prep in advance and what we should show them how to do."

"Remember they are beginners and younger

than us. They will be more high maintenance," Ava said as she walked away from me.

That statement makes no sense. Again, keeping it to myself.

As I got everything set up and ready on our end, Bradley managed Ava while he set up. He was incredibly patient with her. Those two had come a long way since he was in love with her and she snubbed him for his sister Delilah. But Bradley had his own issues right now with Lydia.

"Okay, you two, time to get your body mics on," Bradley said reaching for Ava's chest.

Ava slapped his hand away, "Huh-uh, mister— you and I have had this conversation before. I don't go that way!"

Bradley, with his clean-shaven, boyish looks appeared amused. "I need to attach this microphone on your shirt, Ava. It will make it a lot easier for the students to hear you both."

"Oh, okay, I guess that's okay." Ava said, relaxing a bit but still keeping an eye on him.

We got everything set up, and I put my cat apron on to get ready and go. The apron was beige with different cartoon cats doing multiple tasks in the kitchen.

"You are not wearing that, are you?" Ava almost gagged from disgust.

"Seriously, gag reflex because I have my cute cat apron on? What is wrong with you?"

"It's just goofy. You want them to take us seriously, right? You are the one who said we need to be professional."

"It's an apron. I'm cooking. I had a little bit I was going to say to the students about finding a cool apron that suits them to have fun while cooking. It's a good thing you are getting this out of your system now before we are on camera."

"Did you just describe that as cool?"

Bradley cleared his throat loudly.

Ava and I bug-eyed him.

"I was flailing my arms over here. You two, the session has started, and you are on air. You should be able to see everyone, and they can see and hear you!" Bradley whisper-yelled at us.

I looked at the computer like a deer in headlights. I willed my body not to go slack while holding my head high to maintain some type of composure.

Ava, on the other hand, went into show mode.

"Oh, my goodness, look at all you beautiful cooks! You look amazing! We are thrilled to have you here!" She glowed from inside out on the camera. Still a little loud and too close. I noticed a few of our students jerk their heads back, but I could tell they loved her enthusiasm.

We got into a flow as we told them a little about ourselves before we started with the cooking lesson.

Ava spent a lot of time talking about her love of the business side of our restaurant, her stylish fashionista outfits and how it was fine for the youth of today to take pictures and share on social media as they wished—so nice of her to give them permission to advertise her look, and her amazing Merengue dance moves. She even included the fact that she was a licensed PI now.

Nothing wrong with a little self-promotion, right?

"Yeah, like, you two ladies have a reputation

around Tri-City for all the crimes you've solved! That is so cool at your age you can still do stuff like that," one dark-haired girl said excitedly.

I felt my chin lower slowly and my eyes narrow at this young woman with long, jet-black hair, but then I reminded myself she was a paying student.

"You know we aren't even thirty, right?" Ava's chin stuck out and hands went on hip. I knew what that meant.

"You know, I'd love to get to know a little about all of you before we get started. I'm going to enable video sharing you guys can see each other and you give us a quick one-minute introduction? We'll all have time to get to know each other more once we get going with the cooking." I said, working to smooth over Ava's anger. Okay, and the sour expression on my face, too. Bradley scooted over to me to quietly show me how to switch to a group conference setting so they could see one another.

"Why don't you start, Darla?" Ava asked the dark-haired queen, glancing at the first one on the stack of the short sign-up forms we had them fill out when they applied for the class. I was grateful that Ava had remembered to print them out. The young lady hopped to her feet and backed up until she was completely visible. She clearly didn't mind being in the spotlight. She wore jeans with big holes over a pair of ripped-up black tights and struck a dramatic theater pose to introduce herself.

"I'm Darla. I go to Triopolis University here in Tri-City where I was born and raised, and I'm majoring in acting. I'm excited to take this course and learn some, like, tips for cooking with cast iron. I figure I'll be a starving artist, so I'll need to learn to cook to save money!" She smoothed her long hair with her hands and then flipped it, sitting back down.

"Thank you! Okay, Alyssa?"

"I'm Alyssa. I plan to major in Graphic Design one day. I spent some time studying your restaurant's website and menu. You have a great branding concept!" Alyssa had short, shaggy, bleach-blonde hair that was very carefree, with pale blue eyes and a porcelain complexion. She wore a heavy sweater even though it was warm outside. I loved her level of professionalism.

"Thank you, and next can we hear from Lahiri?" Ava continued.

"I am Lahiri and I have always been interested in Liberal Arts, focusing on studying the cultural arts. I am from West Bengal, India. My family loves to cook, and they plan to visit at the holiday season. I would like to learn some meals from the U.S. to fix for them to surprise them." Lahiri had deep umber skin and dark brown eyes with straight, shoulder-length shiny dark brown hair. A beautiful, antique-looking hair comb held one side of her hair back. I'd never seen anything like it before. It looked like it was brass, with a delicate, off-white floral design that contrasted her striking thick brown hair.

"And can Mod introduce herself?"

"I'm Mod, I haven't decided on a major yet, but I'm taking different types of classes while I figure it out. I like to do abstract paintings with oils. I wanted to try a cooking class but wanted it to be cheap. This worked." Mod had short red curls, freckles, pale skin, and wore no makeup. She seemed very chill and unruffled.

"And finally, Poppy!" Ava prompted.

"I'm Poppy, and the only way you'll ever know it's me is from this black onyx ring." Poppy held up her hand to the camera to show a silver ring with a large black stone. "I'm working toward being a special effects make-up artist. Actually, every time you see me, I'll look different. I like to experiment on my face." She smiled with pride.

That freaked me out a little and I noticed Ava side-eying me.

"So, that is not what you look like?" Ava asked. I saw Bradley move around to the side out of the view of the camera to get a look at her long straight, mousy-blonde hair. Her cheeks were full like a chipmunk, thin lips, bushy eyebrows, and dark blue eyes. Now I was curious to know what she really looked like.

"So, you all know each other?" I asked, while turning off the group video permissions I had just given them to introduce themselves, so they could hear one another but only see us.

"No, why do you ask?" Lahiri inquired.

"Sounds like you all go to college and are art majors."

"I don't even know what liberal arts means," said Alyssa giggling. "The graphic design I work on ties into advertising and business. I still have to declare a major, though."

"Oh, well, I thought maybe you all were friends and decided to take this class together for fun," I said, feeling silly. I didn't do a four-year college program, so I guess I didn't know what I was talking about. "Anyway, let's get started. The main thing I want you all to remember is safety first. You'll hear this a lot. Cast-iron pans heat up fast and hold their heat. You need to remember *not* to touch the handle of the pan once it's hot. Use an oven mitt, dishtowel, or cast-iron pan handle covers." I held up examples of each as I saw each face nod in agreement.

"When working with oil in the pan," I continued, "it's best to start on a lower heat and raise the heat as needed. If you are new to cooking with cast iron, then always go low and slow first until you get the feel for the correct temperature. You can always use a thermometer to help measure temperature along the way." As I held up a thermometer and began to put it into the oil to demonstrate the amount of time to hold it to figure out the temperature, Ava shook my arm, causing me to drop it in the pan.

"Knock it . . ." I stopped short when I saw her face and noticed she was barely breathing. She was pointing to Alyssa's screen. Bradley was running around from behind the camera to see what was going on as well.

A person in a sinister mask with an upside-down face on it snaked slowly from behind Alyssa. She looked at us, confused by our expressions. My face was frozen, eyes felt like they would pop out of my sockets, I squealed and pointed as Alyssa turned and screamed.

Chapter Two

The figure in the grotesque mask brandished a knife over Alyssa's head, who gasped and cringed away from him.

"NOOOOOOOO!" Bradley lunged to the screen as if he could somehow save her.

Ava covered her eyes, and I watched in shock as the knife disappeared between her ribs. I felt my heart beating in every vein beneath my skin.

"Oh, God, no," I whispered. *Wait. Hold on a second.* I stopped and stared, tilting my head toward the screen, and squishing my eyebrows together. Something was off.

I noticed Bradley and Ava stood at attention too.

"Oh, my God what is happening?"

"What's going on? I can't see anything."

The frightened voices of the students jumbled together. I had permissions set to microphones only—they could hear one another but only see Ava and me, so they could see us panicking but couldn't understand why.

"Alyssa?" I asked, tapping my fist against my lips in nervous anticipation.

"Are you kidding me!?!" Alyssa screamed, standing up and reaching up to hit the masked man in the head.

"GOT YOU!" A man's voice boomed as he pulled the mask off, revealing thick brownish hair with red tints in it.

"Tad, you are so dumb!" Alyssa laughed nervously.

"What's happening?" Darla, the dark-haired beauty asked.

"I have no clue." I sighed and snapped the stove off, realizing no cooking would get done today.

"This is my boyfriend. He's an actor. He is always trying to freak me out!" Alyssa said, swatting at him. "I'm in the middle of an online course, Tad."

"Sorry," he mumbled, grinning and sweeping his floppy hair back off his eyes.

The other students began to realize it was a prank, chattering and laughing with relief..

I was not happy to say the least. I don't know what expression I had on my face, but my face felt flush and I felt my fist squeezing so tightly that my nails were digging into my hands. Normally Ava had zero fear when it came to me, but she must have sensed my outrage.

"Class dismissed. We'll pick back up at same time next week. Alyssa, Jolie and I need to discuss what happened here. We will get back to you."

Alyssa began to protest, but Ava clicked out of the program and closed the laptop.

"That little JERK!" Ava's lip curled as she pounded a fist on my kitchen cabinet.

Frantic meowing came from behind the door to the living room, and little paws scrabbled underneath.

"Bradley, will you unlock the door so the cats can come and go as they please?" I asked. I had a swinging door from the kitchen to the living room, but to do this course, I decided to have a latch temporarily put on so the cats couldn't get in the way or jump on the counter.

"The students are just dumb kids," Bradley said, shaking his head and unlatching the door.

"Do you think Alyssa knew he was going to do that?" I asked. I wanted to believe in her innocence.

"I don't know, but I didn't appreciate that little snide reaction as I was closing the session," Ava huffed.

"Do we need to set more ground rules? I sent a set of rules out through email about paying close attention, taking it seriously, and I had them all sign forms protecting us from things like food allergies or injuries per Niko's suggestions." Niko Mercurio was Leavensport's local attorney and source of information for all things legal.

"Maybe we should check with him. I say make an example of her and refund her fee and then remind the others of the rules and the reasons for them. They're all adults—we aren't their high school teachers, after all," Ava said.

"She's got a point," Bradley said.

My heart sank. Alyssa was the one I liked the most. She had researched us as a successful business model. Uh! "Let's sleep on it first then revisit it in the morning."

Carlos had come in early the next morning to make a

few suggestions for the day's menu, since it was his newfound Mexican theme special.

"So, how'd it go yesterday while Ava and I were gone? Any issues with closing?" I asked.

"None at all, Miss Jolie."

"Carlos, you have worked here for a good while now. You have earned that promotion to assistant manager. Ava and I both have complete trust in you. There is no need for you to call either of us Miss. We are co-workers and friends. Please call me Jolie or I will begin calling you Mr. Carlos."

Carlos laughed and his Woody Woodpecker tee jiggled with glee. He was known to wear nothing but cartoon T-shirts, because he learned to speak English watching cartoons as kid. He still loved to watch them. The kids that came into our restaurant loved his shirts and Carlos was absolutely amazing with the little ones.

"Okay, I call you Jolie and Ava from now on."

"Thank you. Now, you worked all afternoon and all evening yesterday. You didn't have to come in this morning. I could have figured something out."

"I meant to leave notes but forgot. I brought a few recipes that have been popular for you to choose from. I did double-check to make sure we had all the necessary ingredients. Also, I wanted to let you know that I put an order in for Adam's Brew and condiments because we are running low on both."

Man, I don't know how we ever survived without Carlos. He worked so hard and was so passionate about doing a good job. I felt like he put me to shame with his work ethic.

"Hey, Carlos, what is happening?" Ava and Carlos did their special greeting, fist bumping and then a executing a complicated handshake with back-

and-forth hand-slaps, finishing with finger guns.

"Hi Miss Ava—er—I mean Ava. I am heading out but wanted to let . . . Jolie know how last night went." He waved and walked up front to head out.

"Whoa, he called me Ava. Is he mad at us? Did something bad happen last night?" Ava asked.

"No, he's fabulous is what's up. I told him he's management now and we trust him. He is our friend and needs to call us by our first names."

"I've always thought that."

"Me too." I said. "I'm not sure why I didn't insist before now, but he is blowing me away by how great the work he does is. He cares about the business as much as we do."

"Well, we needed some other people to help us out with all this extra stuff we've been taken on the last year," Ava said while checking her phone.

"Waiting on a call?"

"No, I got my new website up and running for the part-time PI work. Bounty-Full Investigative Services Food and Felony Fixes with Sass!" Ava snapped her fingers and shook her head in rhythm while saying the title.

"*All* of that is the title?"

"No silly, don't you know anything about marketing? 'Bounty-Full Investigative Services' is the name of our little company. 'Food and Felony Fixes with Sass!' is the tagline. You *have* to have a tagline!"

"My bad! S-O-R-R-Y! And what exactly do you mean by *our* little company?"

"You've been my sidekick this entire year, so of course you're a part of the business. I've got your name listed in the service section with your contact information. I'm checking to see if we've got any bites yet because I ran an ad on the web locally and had Bradley advertise it in *The Village Herald*," Ava said nonchalantly.

"What? You added my information and advertised it without telling me? Are you insane?" I yelled.

"I didn't think you'd have a cow!"

"Why are you using mom language?"

"I didn't know you would act nuts!"

My shoulders turned to knots. I took a breath. "You know what, if anyone contacts me, I'm directing them to you."

"That's fine for now, while you get the hang of it all. Geesh!" Ava rolled her eyes at me.

Sometimes I felt like my head would explode. Fighting Ava was a losing battle.

"Oh, I need to run into the city soon," Ava added. "Do you remember Peggy, from Peggy's Pies and Purses?"

"Yep."

"Her neighbor has a business called Gemma's Bohemian Jewelry and I guess Gemma is a whiz at marketing. Peggy told me I should meet her to get some great tips on marketing for the new business. I figured we could drive up that way together and maybe get some info that can help with Cast Iron Creations, too."

"I don't know that we need to waste money on advertising, Ava. We're in a small town and have a regular customer base. Plus, we do so much cross-selling and now starting this online cast iron course—that's advertisement in itself."

"Hey, we'd get to enjoy some good pie, check out purses and jewelry, and get some free marketing advice."

"You're right, sounds like a fun afternoon!"

Ava headed to the office to set up our marketing outing and I grabbed some to-go boxes to take up front for the baked goods we had prepped for that day.

Lydia walked in, sporting black leggings and a short-sleeved green maternity shirt. I hated to admit it, but pregnancy looked good on her. Lydia was short with straight, shoulder-length blonde hair, bangs, and sparkling eyes that always had fire in them. She always looked ready to rumble, especially with me.

I watched her bend down to pet Spy, chatting with Mirabelle for a few minutes. Lydia was a beautiful woman and while we didn't always see eye-to-eye, she was a decent person.

"Hello, Jolie," she said crisply, strolling to the counter.

"How can I help you today?" I was completely professional while trying not to stare at the baby bump as I wondered if she had slept with Meiser.

"Well, me and little Micky here have a craving for some of those cast iron donuts you fry up. Can I get a dozen to go, please?" She looked down at her belly, rubbing it affectionately.

"You already know the sex of the baby?" Ava asked, walking out from behind the kitchen door, and putting a hand on my arm. She had obviously heard the "Micky" comment.

I sucked in a lot of air and hadn't exhaled yet.

"Yes, *we* just found out the other day. Isn't it wonderful?" She giggled, continuing to rub her tummy.

"Who is 'we'?" I asked through gritted teeth.

"Well, I don't think I'll gossip about it."

"You look like the cat that just ate the rat!" Ava bellowed.

"Canary," I said.

"Huh?"

"You mean I look like the cat that ate the canary," Lydia agreed.

"Why would a cat eat a canary that is tiny and no meat on it when it could just as easily eat a big fat rat?"

My head started to hurt. "You get her drift, Lydia. You're goading me. I heard the gossip that was spreading around at my birthday celebration. It's either Keith's, Bradley's, or Mick's—and you just said the name of the little boy. So, either you are blatantly lying to get a reaction, or you and Mick went together to find out the gender."

Lydia grinned.

Ava pulled out her phone and started dialing.

"What are you doing?" Lydia demanded with puffed-out red cheeks and fire in those sea-green eyes.

"I'm calling Meiser right now to ask him if he went with you," Ava said, dialing.

I smirked to myself. I wasn't going to stop her.

"Put it down," Lydia slapped at Ava's phone then bent over and yelled in pain, grabbing her side.

"I'm not buying it!" Ava yelled.

I didn't want to chance it. "Hang up, Ava."

Waddling to a table, Lydia eased herself into a chair with a worried look on her face.

"Do you need me to call someone?" I asked.

Lydia glared at me. "I can't control if you call Mick."

Rolling my eyes, I said, "That's not what I meant. I can call your doctor. I was just trying to help you, Lydia."

She looked down at the floor. "I just need to sit here a minute. He's kicking, that's all, but he's kicking hard."

Just then, who would walk into the restaurant, but Mick. He was smiling and walking toward me until his eyes focused on Lydia hunched over in the chair. "What happened?" He moved quickly to her, kneeling beside her.

"I came in to buy some donuts, and Ava and Jolie ganged up on me about the father of the baby. Ava went to call you and I started cramping or he started kicking. Anyway, I just had to sit for a minute. I'm fine now."

He stood and held a hand out to help her up. I was speechless, and my mouth was hanging open.

"We ganged up on YOU?" Ava asked incredulously.

"Not the time, Ava," Meiser said flatly.

Ava had that look. I grabbed her arm, knowing we would not win this battle. Mick had his arm around Lydia as he led her out the door.

At that moment, my phone buzzed. I looked down to see a text from Delilah.

If Ava is there, please don't let her know it's me. Can you come to the arts-and-crafts room so we can talk without Ava knowing?

"Is that Mick apologizing?" Ava grunted.

"It's family. I have to go out for a few minutes. I'll be back soon," I said, not wanting to lie to her and considering Delilah family—so, it was a small fib.

Ava grabbed my elbow with a worried look. "Anything wrong?"

I shook my head, thinking of a quick excuse. "Not unless being annoying counts. Just the usual."

She smirked. "Well enjoy."

Delilah was pacing in her tiny office when I walked in and one of her staff pointed to where she was. This felt off.

"What's up?" I asked, concerned.

"I need to tell you something." She took a deep breath. "I know this isn't fair, but I don't want you to tell Ava. So, if that will not work for you then I'll keep it to myself."

I hesitated to think about that. While Ava and I acted more like siblings (and at times sibling rivals) than best friends, the thing that made our relationship work so well is that we have always been brutally honest with one another.

"You are like family now. I want to help, but what you tell me will help me determine what is best for Ava. While I love you too, my loyalty is to her first. And I'm sorry if that is hurtful."

Running her delicate hand through her long wavy locks, Delilah looked tortured in what to do.

"Seems like you should tell me, and I can help decide if Ava should know or not," I prompted.

Taking a deep breath, Delilah blurted quickly, "You know Thiago paid everyone back from the blackmailing in the DR—me included. He even wrote me a beautiful letter welcoming me into the family, and apologizing for meeting me under such horrible circumstances and putting my business in jeopardy. I tried to use that money to buy back my shares of the gallery from Nestle, but he refuses to sell. I don't know why, but I have a strong feeling it is not for a good reason. I'm worried."

"Wow, what is this guy's problem? It's like he's out to destroy our town. Why are you afraid to talk to Ava about all this?"

"You know Ava is not one to get embarrassed, but she hates it when anyone brings up last February. I think she feels ashamed, which is ridiculous. Plus, I'm worried what she may do about Nestle. That is my biggest concern. I get the feeling he is not one to mess with. You know as well as I do that Ava will try to go head-to-head with him."

Giving that some thought I said, "Okay, I agree for now we don't let Ava in on it. Let me do some looking into him and see if I can get an idea of why he is doing this. We are going to tell her, though. We just need more information first."

I sat in Tabitha's office, sharing more about what I've learned the last several months, especially after being in the Dominican Republic for a month. I stared at the new piece of art Tabitha had on her wall—a rendering of a woman in boxing shorts and a sports bra, working out with a kickboxing bag. The entire piece was done in charcoal, except the bag which looked like red oil paint.

Besides being a rough-around-the-edges, at times brutally honest therapist, Tabitha was also a powerhouse kick boxer. I wasn't thrilled with her at first, but with time, I grew to respect and appreciate her unique perspective as a therapist and have found how well it works for me.

"It seems like the time away from Leavensport really gave you a different perspective. You have grown more in a few months than the entire last year we've worked together. Do you agree or disagree?" Tabitha studied my face.

"Both. I did learn a lot about myself, what I want moving forward, and that I am the one who needs to make things happen. It's difficult to figure out exactly how to do that, though." I frowned.

"Why?"

"Maybe that's not the right way to say it. It's not difficult for me to figure out what I want and how to do it in my head, but when it comes time to do it—put it to action—that is when it is difficult."

"Example?"

"Meiser and I. We talked on the phone the entire time I was there. We said we'd talk when I returned. Just the two of us. I got back, saw him with Lydia, and then he disappeared. He returns and we are right back to being awkward and avoiding each other while still running into each other and being vague about things."

"Life doesn't work the way we see it in our heads, Jolie. Life is chaotic and messy. You can't categorize life and separate the good and the bad. It all rests next to each other—the ugly things and the great things sit right next to each other and cozy up to each other."

"But you've been telling me to figure things out. I have to do it in my mind first."

"Most people do. You aren't wrong. It looks one way in our mind—most of the time like a good book or a TV show. Doing it is an entirely different story."

"That's what I'm afraid of. It won't end up the way I want it to."

"What do you want?"

"I don't know anymore. I wanted to have that talk and be completely honest. I wanted to start dating again. I wanted for us to get married, then to start a family. I figured that all out in the DR and I was excited to get back to start a new life."

"Then life threw you a curveball," Tabitha stood up and moved to her desk, opening a drawer.

"Exactly, and yes, I can now tell him I want to talk, but I don't feel the same about him that I did before. At least I don't think I do anymore."

Tabitha handed me a book. I looked at the cover. *Girl, Wash Your Face* by Rachel Hollis.

"This is a great book," Tabitha assured me. "The author talks about what she wants, and how she has felt like everyone but her has their lives figured out. She opens up about the messiness of her own life while pushing through to get where she wants to be."

"Thank you, sounds a lot like me."

"It's a bestseller because so many women relate to this, Jolie. You are right in that you have an ending in your head, but the universe, life, a higher power—whatever you believe, may have a different path for you. Life is about adjustment and choices. You have little control, but you always do have choices for navigating life."

"Wow, this has all been eye-opening. I will be reading this soon."

"We'll talk more after you read it."

Heading to my car, I saw Bradley and Keith in what looked like a heated argument. It was safe to assume it was about Lydia. Unfortunately, I was about to find out firsthand, since they were standing on the sidewalk right next to my car.

"Why don't you get it through your thick, brawny jock skull that you shouldn't have gone after my girl? I'm a nerd? If I'm such a nerd, then why does Mr. Stud Muffin have to chase after my leftovers?" Bradley's face was beet red and spit was flying out of his mouth as he screamed in Keith's face.

Keith lunged forward and simultaneously made a fist, pulling his arm back to swing.

Instinctively, I shut my eyes tightly and did a scootchy walk in between the two men who towered over me in anger. I flailed my arms around my head, yelling, "Not my face, boys! Don't hit the money maker!" I cringed, waiting for an accidental punch, but continued to scoot and flail with eyes closed.

Nothing. I stopped and hesitantly peeked out of one eye on the side of Keith who was standing dead still, smirking.

I opened both eyes and Bradley had air puckered up in his cheeks. He looked at Keith, and they both exploded in laughter at the same time.

"Oh, okay, I get it. I'm the court jester. So extremely happy to entertain you both!" I stomped to my car. I unlocked it and was halfway inside when I stopped mid-squat, and yelled at the two laughing goons, "AND, YOU ARE BOTH WELCOME FOR STOPPING YOUR BRAWL!"

Chapter Three

"Do you like it?" Mick asked me from across the table in his Italian restaurant. He looked well-groomed in a white pinstripe button-down shirt and with a freshly shaven jaw line.

A forkful of chocolate souffle was transmitting pure sugar joy from my tongue to my brain. I smiled slowly. Everything seemed hazy.

"I can't ..." I paused to swallow, my mind caught in slow motion, "even remember ..." I put another bite into my mouth and sighed, talking with my mouth full, "why I was so mad at you ..."

BEEP BEEP BEEP BEEP

The scene dissolved as I was yanked back into the real world. Morning peeked through my curtains. I was wrapped in blankets and buttressed by warm, sleeping furballs. I didn't want to move. Suddenly, everything that had happened in the last few days came flooding into my brain. Mick's possible affection for Lydia. The online cooking class's rocky start. Bradley and Keith's argument on the sidewalk the day before, and my clownish act.

My stomach plunged with anxiety. *I can't do it. I just can't do it. Not today. No.* I squeezed my eyes shut, trying to pretend this day wasn't happening.

Then a thought struck me. I could take a day off. Carlos had shown repeatedly that he could handle things without me, and Ava would be there ... I felt myself relax. *I deserve a day to myself. I'm doing this for me.*

I pulled the blanket up to my chin and snuggled into my pillow. I was beginning to drift off when, suddenly, a weight pressed down on my chest and stomach. My eyes flew open. *Reeeooooowwww? Reeeeoooooowwww?* Bobbi Jo stared down at me expectantly, her little bobtail wiggling with impatience.

"Right, right, sorry," I mumbled, hobbling down the stairs with my blanket around my shoulders and trailing behind me like an old-fashioned bridal train. I managed to feed kitties and scoop litter with one hand since the other was busy clutching my majestic cape.

"No sleeping in for Mommy, huh?" I cooed to Lenny, who was purring his gratitude and rubbing against my legs. "Not even on her day off?" I gave up and chucked the blanket onto the back of a kitchen chair. "It's okay, I'm hungry anyway." But for what? Something indulgent but low effort. Something with chocolate, but still breakfast-y. Chocolate chip pancakes? No. I knew just the thing.

I snapped the oven on to preheat to 425 degrees, then beat a single egg for an egg wash. Once the oven beeped that it was hot enough, I pulled some leftover store-bought puff pastry out of the fridge. *Pain au chocolate* would hit the spot. Well, the Jolie version of it. It was supposed to be a delicate puff pastry with one or two small pieces of dark chocolate in the center. I pulled a full-sized Hershey bar out of the pantry and wrapped the puff pastry around it, brushing the outside with the egg wash and popping it into the oven. The French would be so appalled. I giggled.

While my breakfast treat baked, I collected blankets and books, piling them on the couch. It would be my fortress of comfort for the day. I clicked on the television and flipped through the channels. Rom-com? No, thank you. I didn't want to think about love. Ahh, a black-and-white detective movie. Perfect. I had just started to smell something glorious from the oven when my phone rang. *Ava.* I declined the call. *Sorry, friend. Not today. She'll figure it out eventually.*

I opened the oven and pulled out the rack. The pastry had morphed into a flaky golden volcano, with rivulets of molten chocolate pouring out. I slid the whole thing into a large ceramic serving bowl and grabbed a fork. I was glad no one else was here to watch me devour this thing. It was not going to be dignified.

I settled onto the couch with the detective movie on the television and the book Tabitha lent me propped up against the bowl in my lap. Sammy Jr. had turned into a perfectly round, furry cushion that rested, vibrating, on my shins. Bobbi Jo was stretched out on the back of the couch like a lion on the savanna. Lenny was perched right next to me, on the arm of the couch. DJ was nowhere to be seen, so probably eating or breaking something.

I took a huge bite of my breakfast pastry. Chocolate dribbled down my chin. *Oh man, that was good.*

An hour later, I was fifty pages into my book, two-thirds of the way through my French Chocolate Volcano, and the square-jawed detective on the screen was in a taxi, heading to the cabaret to ask the owner some very pointed questions about his whereabouts at eleven p.m. last Thursday. I had very nearly forgotten my troubles.

At least, until my front door slammed open and a small crowd of people poured through it: my Aunt Fern, my mother Patty, Uncle Wylie, Grandma Opal and her boyfriend Tom, with my cousin Tink and Ava bringing up the rear.

A lot of very interesting words came out of my mouth.

"Jolie!" shrilled my mother, her eyes enormous. I leapt to my feet, sending cats scampering.

"You I get." I pointed at Ava's chest. "You get a pass for bursting in here." I whirled on the rest of them. "But why, in the name of the Fourth Amendment, is my entire family, including my grandmother's boyfriend, IN MY HOUSE?"

Uncle Wylie elbowed Aunt Fern. "Which one's the Fourth Amendment?"

"The right to privacy," sighed Aunt Fern. "She's got herself a smart mouth."

"Privacy, pshaw!" snorted Grandma Opal. Only my grannie would *pshaw* the US Constitution. She'd probably *pshaw* James Madison himself. Or flirt with him. I felt a chortle rise in my chest.

"Just look at her with that weird smile on her face," clucked my mother Patty. "Mick went and broke her heart and now she's losing it. It's a good thing we came over when we did."

My anger boiled back up in an instant. "That's why you're here?"

"Now, sweetie," said Grandma, "I was out shopping, and everyone was whispering about how Mick could be the father of Lydia's baby! After what she had said at the party, and then all the gossip, it was just too much. So, I rushed right over to the restaurant to tell you, but Ava said you weren't there and weren't answering your phone!" She paused to take a breath. "What were we *supposed* to do?"

I was so angry my hands were shaking and my breath was coming in ragged gasps. I was pretty sure my face was beet red.

"Hey!" I shouted, startling everyone. "My life is not an open cardboard box at some yard sale that everyone is allowed to wander past and root around in as they please. I don't appreciate that every move I make is headline news on the Tucker Family News Channel. Also, I know that you all know! Ava already told me!" My hands were clenched in fists and my jaw was clamped hard.

"Jolie, honey," said my mother in a syrupy voice, "we do all of that because we care about you. You know that. We tried to leave you alone, even after what Lydia said at the party, but you didn't contact us. You left us no choice."

My shoulders slumped and I sank back down onto the couch. I looked down at the remnants of my French Chocolate Volcano, languishing in the bowl. It was crumpled and deflated, just the way I felt. This was the part of the argument where I always gave up. They are my family. Their hearts are in the right place, even if their execution is a bit

... clumsy. Tears sprang to my eyes.

I imagined telling Tabitha about this familial home invasion at my next session. Today would certainly not go down in history as a victory. This thought grounded me and gave me strength. I took a deep breath. *You can do this, Jolie.* I stood back up and turned to face them.

"I apologize for yelling," I said in a steady voice. "However, I do need all of you to listen. I have something important to say." They had been milling around, murmuring among themselves, but they fell silent. "I know that all of you care about me, and that this—" I gestured around myself, "was intended as an act of kindness, but it has to stop. I am going to set some boundaries. And you guys are going to respect them."

My family looked perplexed. Tom, Grandma's boyfriend, stared awkwardly out of the window with his hands behind his back. Tink had wandered off to the kitchen to play with Lenny.

"First and foremost, you may only come to my house when I invite you over. Please do not show up unannounced. Please do not use whatever extra copies of keys you have made over the years to let yourselves in." My mom and Grandma Opal began to make little squawks of protest. Uncle Wylie gently shushed them, tipping his head toward me as if to say, *Let's listen to what she has to say.* I knew everything I was saying was in vain. They would continue to butt into my life. Baby steps for us all.

"What if we want to see you?" demanded Aunt Fern.

"Call or message me with an invitation to come to *your* house," I suggested. My family looked at one another.

"Moving on." I was feeling good about this. I was getting so much off my chest. "Please do not ... intervene ... in my romantic relationships. Don't follow my exes, don't call them, don't confront anyone on my behalf, don't try to set me up with anyone new. All of that is my own private business." Again, this was a hope, but I knew better. But they needed to hear it.

"If the whole town is gossiping about someone you're in a relationship with, we're just supposed to . . ." Grandma Opal seemed literally unable to finish the sentence.

"Just keep it to yourself. You were able to give me space for a while. Stretch it out longer!" My voice was gentle but firm. "Any questions?"

"No," my mom said stiffly. "I think we're clear."

"Great," I said, ignoring her tone. "Now, if you will excuse me, I want to start preparing for next week's online cooking class." Everyone filed out of the front door. Uncle Wylie gave me a smile and a quick wave on the way out. Tink gave the cats one last pat and joined them. Ava was almost out the door when I grabbed her arm.

"Not you!" I said. Ava looked relieved and plopped down on a kitchen chair. The door closed.

"So ..." Ava said cautiously. "Wow."

"Yeah, wow," I agreed.

"Do you think they'll abide by your wishes?"

"I really don't know." I stared out of the window for a moment. "We'll have to see. But I have to stick to my guns. I need boundaries."

Ava snuck a look at me. "May *I* ask what your thoughts are on this whole Lydia and Mick thing?"

"Nope," I shook my head. "We have other

things to worry about right now. What are we going to do about Alyssa?"

"I have worked with some of Delilah's adult art students on a few projects." Ava shook her head. "They love to socialize. They love to get attention—actors. Sometimes they don't know when to take things seriously. If we let it slide, our class might turn into a variety show. It seems harsh, but I think we should refund her money and expel her from the class. Make an example of her."

"I feel bad penalizing her, since we don't know if that was something she planned with him or if he was just playing a prank on her." I furrowed my brow. "But Poppy, Mod, Lahiri, and Darla paid to learn about cast iron cooking."

"If we are kicking her out, we should call her and let her know right away," Ava concluded. "We don't want her thinking all week she is still in the class. Plus, we need to decide if we want to find a replacement."

"Yeah, okay, you're right. We can't let this class go off the rails," I finally agreed. "I'll call her. Then we need to map out the lesson. You know I like to prepare in advance and make changes throughout the week." I reached for my phone to deliver the bad news. "I want this next class session to be a well-oiled machine."

Alyssa's number rang twice before she picked up. I heard her talking to someone in the background. "No, I think it's my cooking class, hold on."

"Hi, Alyssa, it's Jolie Tucker," I said, my stomach twisting with nervousness.

"Hello," she replied. "What can I do for you?"

"Well, I am sorry to say that I have some bad

news. We have a ... zero tolerance policy ..." I was flailing, trying to find professional sounding reasons for our decision. I definitely should have scripted this out before I called. "for behavior ... in class ... that is disruptive, violent, or ..." Ava shoved something scribbled on a napkin at me to read: *induces panic.* "... induces panic," I finished. "We are going to have to expel you from our cooking class, but we will provide a full refund," I concluded, trying to end on a positive note.

"Are you serious?" All of the professionalism drained out of Alyssa's voice. "You're going to kick me out of a class because of a dumb joke?" She was shouting now. "I can't control what my boyfriend does! You can't hold me responsible for that. This is ridiculous! You guys are such jerks!" Without another word, she hung up. I lowered the phone and looked at Ava, who had one eyebrow quirked.

"That went about as well as could be expected," I sighed. "Let's plan out next week's class session, shall we?"

Ava got out a notebook and began to write out a lesson plan and I made a list of supplies we would need to pick us later in the week to teach the class. We thought it would be clever to teach our way through a steak dinner. We wanted to cover a soup as an appetizer, two side dishes, a steak, and a dessert, all made in cast iron.

Being as this would be the first full class period, we were planning to teach them the lesson how to make cast iron skillet creamy potato soup that was intended for the first class, but we still needed to plan the rest of the course.

We liked to make the food in advance to rehearse and work through possible problems. So, we'd go buy the groceries today and probably make the soup tonight to prepare.

"Okay," I stood up and grabbed my list. "I'm going to get dressed and get ready for the day!" Ava stood up and leaned over my shoulder, studying the slip of paper.

"This seems pretty simple and hard to mess up. Why don't you let me do the supply run?" she offered.

I looked sideways at her. "You never go to the grocery store. Why today?"

"I mean, you were trying to take a mental health day and that got messed up, and I kind of feel like it was maybe a little bit my fault." Ava shrugged. "You could relax for a few hours before we do our trial run on the soup. I kind of wanted to stop by and see Delilah anyway."

"Sold!"

I was snuggled on the couch with the TV on before Ava was even out the door. I must have drifted off to sleep, because I woke to my phone buzzing against my face like a large rectangular insect. I picked up before I was even fully aware of what was happening.

"Hello?" I mumbled.

"Hello? Miss Tucker?"

"Wait. Alyssa?" I snapped awake.

"... yeah, it's me." Her voice was soft and uncertain, like she was embarrassed. "Listen, I know you aren't going to let me back in the class. That isn't why I'm calling. I just wanted to apologize to you for being so rude earlier."

"Well, thank you for that, Alyssa." I cleared my throat. "I know what I said wasn't easy to hear."

"Yeah, I didn't want to burn bridges with you. I was hoping ..." she took a deep breath, "if you keep teaching online classes ... maybe at some point I could sign up for one of your classes again? I am really interested in cooking and I like your style. It's inspiring. So independent and confident. You are a real role model for young female entrepreneurs." She sounded a little teary. "You're a role model for me, actually. Which is why I was so excited to take your class. And so angry when I got kicked out." Alyssa sniffed.

I was floored. I was a role model? I could change this kid's life.

"Listen, Alyssa." Words were coming out of my mouth before I knew what I was saying. "First of all, you can call me Jolie if you want. I want to give you a second chance. Can you have a talk with your boyfriend, what's his name?"

"Tad."

"Yes, Tad. Can you have a talk with him and tell him no more theatrics?"

"I sure can, Jolie!" squealed Alyssa. "Thank you so much! I'll be there next class!"

"I'll see you then." I hung up the phone. I trusted her to fix her behavior. But what on earth was Ava going to say about this?

Ava and I walked into Peggy's Pies and Purses, grinning ear to ear from the old-time diner appearance, the wonderful smells of pies, and seeing Peggy with her long, wavy strawberry-blonde pigtails, lanky legs in jeggings with soft high-top tennis shoes and a yellow and white checkered half shirt. She was adorable and fit the old-fashioned look of her little diner.

"I've missed you both SO much!" Peggy shouted in glee, running to grab us both in a big bear hug.

"You just saw me a few weeks ago," Ava giggled.

"I know, but I haven't seen this one in ages!" She pointed her fresh face in my direction. "Now, have a seat, I just texted Gemma when I saw you two walking in, she'll be right over."

Peggy went behind the counter and came back with a tray of pie samples. There was coconut cream, chocolate cream, sugar cream, blueberry, apple, cherry, Dutch apple, and Oreo iced cream pie. My mouth watered.

"Oh man, what are all of you going to have?" A beautiful woman with harvest moon, sepia skin said. She had long, thick dreadlocks that came to her waist with the coolest bright-colored beads at the bottom of her dreads. She wore a maroon head scarf with yellow, green, and white fan shapes. I noticed she had on funky jewelry including bright green and black beaded necklaces, multi-colored, beaded bracelets on each arm, and emerald, sapphire, and pearl rings covering her fingers.

We all laughed as Peggy introduced us to Gemma.

"Hey, that was my line!" Ava bellowed reaching out a hand to shake.

We all reached for sample pies and dug in as Gemma asked Ava how the marketing tips she gave her were going.

"It's going good so far. I've got the website up

and running with our contact information on it. My girlfriend, Delilah, made some flyers, too." Ava reached into her bag pulling out several and handing them to Peggy and Gemma. "There are two separate flyers for each of you—one for our online courses for later in the year to register and one for the PI business. I appreciate you both helping to spread the word in the city."

"Of course, our pleasure." Peggy got up and went and grabbed some tape and put one of each on her door and then tacked one of each up on her bulletin board by the cash register.

"I'll do the same in my store," Gemma said. "Oh man, guess what? Your mayor was in my shop yesterday!"

Ava and I looked at each other in shock. "Mayor Nalini? What was he doing here?" I exclaimed.

Gemma's eyebrows waggled up and down. "He asked me what kind of jewelry a lovely lady might like to wear. I sold him a pair of teardrop moonstone earrings. I wonder who he was buying them for?"

"Who knows? I didn't realize he was dating!" Ava said. Our mayor was one of several eligible bachelors in Leavensport.

The diner was set up so that customers walked into the pie shop but there was an entrance to the back that led to the purse shop. Gemma's jewelry store was located right next door.

We finished our pies and went to check out the purses in the back. Our final destination would be the jewelry store. I was examining a brown leather tote that looked similar to the one I was carrying when I heard a familiar voice up front. I noticed

Ava caught my eye in the same moment.

"Is that—" Ava started as we both moved toward the beaded curtain that separated the front and back, which I was sure was made by Gemma. We pushed the long-beaded strings to the side in time to see Tad, Alyssa, Darla, Lahiri, Mod, and another girl I'd never seen before—could that be Poppy–all out front chatting it up and laughing. They had another man with them. He looked a bit older than they were, and wore a large, black-and-white-checkered kerchief around his neck. It made me think of a director. None of them noticed that we were watching them. My head spun. *Those little liars!*

"The girl with the bleach blonde silky bob, is that Poppy?" I asked Ava.

"Probably, I'm not sure how much that one can be trusted—she's good at altering her appearance—for all we know Peggy or Gemma could be Poppy in disguise."

That made my stomach turn.

"Should we say something?" I asked Ava.

She pulled me back from the curtains. "Peggy, do you know those kids up front?"

Peggy looked perplexed and looked up front then walked over to where we had hidden ourselves behind the wall. "I don't know them, but they come in here pretty regularly. They got to Triopolis University. It's not far from here. They can easily walk depending on where they live on campus."

"So, they come in here as a group?" I asked.

"Normally if you see one, you see them all," she said then went off to answer a question for a customer.

"So, the little twerps *do* know each other!" Ava crossed her arms.

"Looks that way. I say we don't call them on it. We should have guessed, though. They are all the same age. They are all majoring in something artsy. Well, except Mod, but she mentioned she likes to paint. Why would they lie? I asked them point blank and they lied to us."

"Maybe they were worried we wouldn't think they would take the class seriously? If we knew they were a bunch of friends?"

"What?" I said sarcastically. "Act like fools in our class? NEVER!"

"Point taken. Let's see what happens at our class next week."

I'll keep an eye out the window and come out and help you unload when you get here.

It was time for the next class. Last week was a whirlwind of prepping for this week's class, plus we had been extra busy at the restaurant since Carlos had to take several days off when he caught a spring cold, and I had to keep my family under control after giving them the third degree.

I sent the text and went back to scrunching my hair. I had gotten out of the shower and put in leave-in conditioner fifteen minutes ago and now it was time for the all-important finger fluffing that makes my curly hair presentable.

Although technically, I was only an honorary curly-haired person. Every few months I got a perm to keep my hair looking like my BFF Ava's natural curls. We had been a pair of curly tops for as long as I could remember.

I swiped on some mascara and lip gloss and put some cat-shaped silver studs in my ears. I heard her pull up in the driveway, so I went out to help.

Since Ava did the shopping last week, she volunteered to go again for tonight's class. Ava was trying to carry everything from her trunk into the kitchen in one trip. She had four plastic grocery bags on each arm, the handles cutting into her forearms. I took two from each arm and we tottered into the house together.

We bustled around, arranging the show area. Bradley came in and began setting up his equipment. He waved hello in our direction but wouldn't make eye contact with me. I tried to peek at his face to see if he had any bruises. I wondered if, after all the laughing stopped last week, they decided to beat each other to a pulp anyway. I hadn't seen either of them since.

I chopped up and arranged the ingredients into ramekins and wrote out the recipe on the white board, trying to find the right time to tell Ava about my decision to let Alyssa stay in the class. Things were about to start, though, and she needed to know. No time like the present!

Bradley put on some headphones. "Just talk for a little while in a normal voice while I adjust the levels." I gave him a thumbs up.

"Oh, hey, forgot to tell you!" Ava said to me. "I ran into Bea at the grocery store."

"Bea Seevers?" I asked. "How is she?" I took a swig of water from my water bottle.

"I started telling her about our online cooking class and she thought it was really cool. She said she was interested in learning to do more with cast iron cooking, so I offered her the open spot in our class! I sent her the link and everything. She'll be in class today!" She beamed at me.

I gasped as I was drinking, inhaling water. I coughed and choked for a few seconds while Ava thumped me on the back. Bradley ripped his headphones off and grabbed his ears, glaring at us. Apparently, our coughing and back-thumping was super loud on the body mics. I waved a one-armed apology while I struggled for air.

"Are you okay?" asked Ava.

"Yeah," I croaked, realizing maybe I should have told Ava sooner rather than later. "But I may have screwed up." She looked alarmed. "Alyssa called back after you left last week to pick up groceries and apologized. She seemed really sincere and genuinely interested in cooking. She promised everything would be smooth sailing from now on ... so I told her she could come back to class." I looked guiltily at Ava. Her eyes widened for a second, and then she laughed.

"That is totally something we would do," Ava laughed. "Give one class spot to two people. I don't think it is a problem, though. It just means we have six people in our class instead of five. We can handle that."

"Yeah," I agreed, "we can handle one more person for sure, especially a well-behaved one like Mrs. Seevers." We chuckled at the thought of little old Bea causing trouble in our class.

"Speaking of, though," Ava said, furrowing her brow, "Alyssa better keep her attitude to herself. I've got my eye on her."

"She promised she would," I reassured her.

The kitchen was set up and the ingredients were ready. Ava and I turned to one another and checked each other's hair and makeup one last time. We smiled at each other. I was excited. This time, our class would be perfect!

"Okay, ladies, the class starts in ten," called Bradley while doing a two-handed countdown from nine, eight, and so on. We stood in our places, watching his fingers until he hit one. He waved to us, and we turned and smiled at the camera.

"Oh my goodness, look at all you beautiful cooks! You look amazing! We are thrilled to have you here!" said Ava, using the same introduction she had used for the first session. I grinned. She wasn't letting on that we knew what liars they were.

"Now, I emailed everyone the list of ingredients for today's dish," I began, smiling at the camera, "and I hope everyone has everything out in their workspace, ready to go." I gestured with my hands at our countertop, which was covered with ramekins, cutting boards, and utensils. "But first, we have some class housekeeping to take care of."

I glanced at Ava, who nodded at me.

"I would like to welcome a new student, Bea, to our class. Everyone, say hello to Bea!" I peeked at the monitor that showed the faces of all of the students in a grid. I saw the chat filling up with comments of "Hello!" and "Welcome to our class!"

The students' cameras didn't come on until the class started, so this was the first time I had a chance to see them this session. Mrs. Seevers had her hair in a tidy bun and was wearing a plaid shirt with the sleeves rolled up. She looked excited but uncertain. I was guessing she wasn't totally comfortable with the technology involved.

Lahiri was grinning, wearing a sporty gray lightweight sweatshirt and her dainty, antique hair comb. Mod was leaning on one hand on her table with her ingredients around her. She wore a plain white V-neck T-shirt, the kind you can buy in a pack of six in the underwear aisle. The careless look worked for her. Alyssa seemed eager to impress, in a nice sweater with a white apron over it. She looked a little bit embarrassed but smiled and waved.

Darla was wearing an elegant top that looked almost Victorian—it was pure white and silky, with a high lace neck, puffed sleeves, and ruffles down the front. Drama majors! My jaw dropped as I glanced at Poppy. Gone was the round-faced blonde. In her place sat a vixen with an electric-blue bob, glossy, blood-red cupid's-bow lips, long, thick eyelashes, and striking cheekbones. I would never have guessed it was the same person. She must have seen me gape on the camera, because she waved her onyx ring and smiled broadly.

"Not bad, huh?" she said.

"You're really good at changing your appearance!" I exclaimed. "Wow! Okay, folks, let's get started. But first, please make sure your cast-iron skillet and your cast-iron Dutch oven are preheating over medium heat, so they'll be ready. Now, I just want to remind everyone that it is important to maintain proper classroom behavior during these sessions. This will help us get through the material during the class period, and also keep you guys safe. We are working with sharp knives, hot stoves, and other dangerous kitchen appliances. I would feel terrible if someone got hurt on our watch. Okay?" I saw everyone's head nod on the monitor.

Alyssa looked down at her lap, unwilling to make eye contact in that awkward moment.

"Remember to be careful around hot pans. Don't forget, I recommend using cookware with rubber handles, but if you don't have those, use a pan holder or a thick dishtowel. Safety first!"

"This dish is essentially two recipes put together," Ava said. "It is called 'Crispy Potato Soup' because we are going to create a kind of fried potato garnish that will rest on the top of our creamy potato soup to provide two different textures. If you plan on getting through all three courses of this steak dinner, serve this appetizer in a very small bowl. It is rich!"

"First, chop your uncooked bacon into small pieces and cook it quickly on low to medium heat. You decide how fatty or crispy you want it to be. Be careful!" I instructed. "When the bacon is done to your liking, pull it out with a fork, or, preferably tongs for a better grip. It will end up in the Dutch oven, in the soup, but we'll use the bacon fat to make the crispy potatoes. That's called recycling!" I laughed at my own joke. I was in my element, talking about cooking. I could teach a cooking class to the president.

"If you're vegetarian, there are vegetable protein bacon products you can use for this step," I added. "They won't render any fat out, so you'll need an oil with a high smoke temperature, such as coconut, peanut, or canola." My bacon was done, so I scooped it out with the tongs, transferring it to a paper-towel-lined plate.

"Next," I continued, "we are going to peel and grate one-third of our potatoes and pat them dry with paper towels. The other two thirds will get peeled and cubed." I began to process the potatoes as I talked. "If you would like a thinner soup, be sure to choose a low-starch potato like red potatoes or round white potatoes, or you can soak high-starch potatoes before cooking. If you would like to make a thicker soup, medium or high-starch potatoes are good—Russets. We will be frying some of these, so I asked you folks to get Yukon Golds. They are medium starch and hold shape well when frying, so we get the best of both worlds. Put the vegetables, seasoning, and chicken broth into the Dutch oven and add the cubed potatoes. Cook until the potatoes are tender, probably ten minutes or so." I gave the ingredients a good stir and turned to Ava.

This is the part where Ava and I had rehearsed that she would take over. Cooking wasn't her strong suit, but we had practiced. She stepped up to the counter and picked up a wooden spoon, beaming at our students. I walked off-camera to look at the monitor. Everyone was watching intently, following the directions in their own respective kitchens.

I looked back at the monitor again. Mod had a half-smile on her face as she stirred the potato soup. Poppy's blue wig was slightly askew as she adjusted the heat under her frying potatoes. I could see that Alyssa was taking notes. Lahiri was bent over her Dutch oven, checking her soup. She wiped sweat from her forehead.

I was a little jealous. I had given Ava the fun part of the dish. She was showing them how to set round metal cookie cutters in the bacon-fat-greased cast iron skillet, then fill the cookie cutters with grated potato, using the bottom of a glass to push the potato down. The grated potato would get crispy on the bottom, creating a tasty circle of fried potato that could be placed on top of a small bowl of the creamy potato soup. The finished product was visually appealing and also delicious. As the potatoes fried, Ava gave them a rundown on how to blend their soups into delicious smoothness. I kept a close eye on all of them. It looked like they were all in different places, but I still thought it was strange no one was letting on they knew each other.

"You can use anything from a countertop blender to a good old-fashioned potato masher, but my weapon of choice is an immersion blender." Ava hoisted the well-used one from Cast Iron Creations in the air like Excalibur.

I chuckled. Ava blended the creamy potato soup and ladled it into two bowls, placed the crispy potato circles on top, and then began garnishing the dish, channeling her girlfriend Delilah's artistic nature and flinging chives, shredded cheddar, and blobs of sour cream everywhere.

Time to review our tips and wrap it up. I was elated. This session was a total success—minus the secrets that no one was sharing!

At that moment, I heard a quiet squeal. My eyes snapped over to the monitor and my blood began to boil. Darla! That was it. No more second chances for anyone.

The dark-haired drama major had turned to face a tall figure in an upside-down face mask exactly like the one Tad had worn. The masked figure had a sharp, dark-metal stake in its hand. In a single gesture, the figure lifted its arm above its head and plunged the stake into Darla's chest.

Darla was a much better actor than Alyssa had been. Her eyes bulged with the shock of being "stabbed." Tad must have invested in fake blood, because it bloomed from the "wound," spreading across her white shirt. Darla grabbed the stake, miming weakly trying to pull it out. Then her eyes became glassy, and she crumpled to the floor and out of sight. The masked figure walked off-camera so quickly it stumbled a little. End scene.

I would have been very impressed by her performance if I wasn't in a blind rage.

"That's it. THAT'S IT!" I roared. I whirled to Bradley, making a cutting gesture across my throat. He killed the camera and ended the session.

Chapter Four

"I mean, Darla was definitely in on that one," growled Ava. "So she's out. I'll call her later."

Suddenly, I was exhausted. "Let's clean this place up. We'll figure everything out tomorrow." We worked in an annoyed silence, then Bradley and Ava waved goodbye and left.

I collapsed at the kitchen table. I peeled the lid off of the container of potato soup that Ava had left with me. I got a few crispy fried potato circles out of the plastic bag and tossed them in, breaking them up with a spoon. I took a bite. I hadn't realized I was so hungry. Wow, that was good. Ava did a great job.

As I ate, my mind began to drift back to what had happened. Darla had obviously planned this gruesome little prank performance, but was she in on the first one, too? We knew she was friends with Tad, and she was also friends with Alyssa. I wondered briefly if Alyssa had helped plan the second performance. Or ... was Tad cheating on Alyssa with Darla? I felt a weird urge to start an I Spy Slides entry for this whole mess, even though no actual crime had been committed. There were so many twists and turns. Especially now that I knew they were keeping secrets.

I sighed. At the very least, we would have to kick Darla out of their class. If we found out that Alyssa was a part of this second escapade, she was out the door, too. Classroom management was way more difficult than I had anticipated.

I put the rest of the potato soup in the fridge and stretched. My bed was calling me. The cats circled my ankles, ready to join me.

My cell started ringing. Not Ava. It was a local number, but not one I recognized. I ignored it. It rang again almost immediately. I groaned and picked up.

"Jolie Tucker?"

"Teddy?" What could he want at this time of night?

"Yes, it's Chief Tobias. Can you confirm that you have a woman named Darla Fredrickson in your online class?"

"Yes, she is one of my students. Why?" I wondered if Ava was so mad she had filed a police report.

"I'm going to need you to come down to the station and answer a few questions about what happened in your class tonight." Suddenly I felt bad. I didn't want Darla to get into legal trouble.

"How about I come down first thing in the morning, Teddy? It wasn't that big of a deal, I promise."

"I need you to come down to the station tonight. Don't make me send an officer out to get you and Ava." said Chief Tobias.

"What are you talking about?"

"Why didn't you call it in immediately?" Teddy demanded.

"Call what in—what are you talking about?"

"Jolie? What do you think I'm talking about? Darla's murder."

Darla's...*murder?*

I am not positive if I said goodbye or not, if I told Teddy I would be there in a few minutes, or if I just hung up on him. I gripped the table edge as the kitchen spun around me. *Not again. Not another murder.* I sank to the chair. Sammy Jr. leapt into my lap and stared into my eyes. His stinky cat food breath brought me back to reality.

"Thanks, Hippy-Toes," I said, scratching behind his ears. Sammy Jr. was so fluffy that he had long black fluff come out of his toes—hence the nick-name. "I needed that. Apparently." He jumped down and wandered away. I pulled on a sweatshirt, grabbed my purse, and headed over to Ava's. Her door flew open before I even knocked. She looked shaken.

"You heard?" She nodded. Without another word we got into her car together. As soon as we arrived, Teddy handed us each a clipboard with a form on it and asked us to write out a statement of what we had seen. A few minutes later, we had both written a few paragraphs and handed them to the young woman sitting at the desk.

Teddy led me to his office and offered me a chair. He sat behind his desk and sighed heavily, rubbing his forehead with his hand.

"We are so sorry, Teddy. You have to know we would never do—whatever you think we did. We weren't in on it. They did a prank last week—we—"

"Wait, who did what last week?" Teddy demanded, then asked, "Is there any chance that you made my life a whole lot simpler by recording tonight's online class?"

I shook my head. "Sorry. The camera is closed circuit, and the conference app doesn't record. I can print out a transcript of everything that was written in the chat if that helps. I'm no techie, but I would guess you could probably get the IP address of the people who were logged in from the app. But, Alyssa, one of our students, has a boyfriend, Tad. They did the same prank—except it was a prank, not a murder." Tears welled up in my eyes.

"I figured. It was a shot in the dark. We'll probably take your laptop for a day or so and see what we can find." I nodded. "Okay," he said finally, "tell me about Darla Fredrickson."

"I don't know much about her, really. She told us that she was a college student, a drama major, at Triopolis University. She seemed nice and didn't cause any problems. We hadn't really gotten far enough into the class to know if she was a good student or not." I stared at my hands.

"And how did she seem in class tonight? Calm? Agitated? Afraid? Distracted?"

"She seemed calm and friendly. She welcomed our new student, Mrs. Seevers. She was participating in class, right up until she was ..." I looked away, shaking my head.

"Did she ever mention anyone she wasn't getting along with, anyone who had threatened her, any sort of trouble she might have been in?" Teddy looked like he knew he was grasping at straws.

"We didn't really get to have those sorts of conversations in class," I explained. "It was more of an 'We teach, they listen/they ask questions, we answer them' situation."

Teddy nodded. "I figured. Just thought I would check." He seemed exhausted. "Listen, can you print out a copy of your class list for me as soon as you can? I need to get a statement from each of them."

"Of course. Um, Chief, can you tell me how you found out about the murder? Ava and I didn't know—like I said—we thought it was a prank." My stomach twisted at the memory.

"One of her housemates found her and called 911," replied Teddy. I wasn't totally sure he was supposed to tell me that. "Everyone knew Darla was taking that class, apparently, and the time of death was after she signed into the conference session on her laptop so there was likely something seen on your end. Now, this is the unpleasant part. Can you tell me exactly what you saw when Darla Fredrickson was killed? I know it is tough, but it could help us catch her killer."

"I looked up because I heard her gasp." I began. I closed my eyes so I could remember as much as I could. "She was standing at the counter of her kitchen where she had been cooking, but she had turned to her left and was facing this tall figure, who was wearing a mask."

"How tall was the figure?"

"I'm not sure. An inch or two taller than Darla."

"Describe the mask, please." Teddy was typing feverishly.

"See, that's the thing, Chief Tobias," I said.

"Whoever stabbed Darla was wearing a mask that was identical to the mask Tad wore during the prank last week. It had an upside-down face on it."

The police chief's eyebrows shot up. He grabbed his radio. "Hey man, you there?" My heart leapt. Meiser was on the case? Of course he was. Why didn't he call me instead of Teddy?

The radio crackled. *Go ahead,* said Meiser's deep voice. I felt my face get pink.

"Keep an eye out for a mask with an upside-down face on it."

Got it, man.

"That is definitely important. Tell me again the name of the boyfriend?" asked Teddy.

"His first name is Tad. It seemed like he lived with Alyssa but I'm not positive. That's the other thing. We found out last week that they all know each other. They acted like they didn't in class."

"And how would you compare the height and build of tonight's attacker to that of Tad?" Teddy watched my face. I wasn't comfortable leading the police toward that kind of conclusion unless I was completely sure. Still, in my mind's eye, the two figures were identical.

"Chief Tobias, I can't really say. They were both tall, but I don't know for sure if they were the same height. I'm sorry I can't be of more help."

Teddy sighed. "Okay. So, what happened after Darla turned and faced the masked attacker?"

"Everything happened really quickly after that." I shuddered. This was the first time I had replayed that scene in my head with the awareness that it was not a prank. "The figure lifted a dark, metal-looking stake above its head and stabbed

Darla right in the heart, on the left side of her chest. She looked confused and started bleeding ..." My eyes blurred with tears. "... Then she collapsed. The masked person waited until she fell down and then walked away from the same direction it had come, to Darla's left."

I took a deep breath and blew my nose as Teddy finished typing. I needed to get my head on straight.

"Well, those are all of my questions for now," he said. Teddy's radio crackled again. *You almost finished? We need you over here.* My ears perked up. Where was "over here"? The scene of the crime?

"On my way," replied Chief Tobias, pulling on his jacket.

Teddy walked me out to where Ava was waiting. "Good night, ladies. Stay safe out there. We'll be in touch."

I grabbed Ava and we hustled to the parking lot. I didn't want to let him get out of my sight. We watched Teddy get into his cruiser and pull out.

"Let him get a little farther up, then follow him!" I said excitely.

"Where are we following him to, exactly?" demanded Ava.

"He's going to Darla's house, the scene of the crime. You're a licensed PI! We can help!"

"If we are going there to help, why are we sneaking?" Ava quirked an eyebrow at me.

"Umm ... force of habit?"

She shook her head but stayed on Teddy's tail at a discreet distance. *She's good at this!*

Teddy signaled and got onto the on ramp to the highway. Ava waited until he was out of sight and then smoothly snapped her headlights off. The moon was bright, but it was still much darker than I preferred. It didn't seem to bother Ava. Hidden by the darkness, she sped up until Teddy's taillights were a manageable distance away. I was in awe.

"You're a natural, Ava!"

She let out a pleased snicker. "Yeah, I know!"

Just minutes later, the police chief turned off onto a small road that terminated in a cul-de-sac of sorts with a ring of large, old, Victorian-style houses. We pulled off and parked where the gravel driveway met the road, but Teddy pulled his police cruiser right up into the center of the houses.

We walked as quietly as we could over crunchy gravel. There were huge oaks and hickories among the houses, and at least a dozen cars parked in seemingly random spots in the driveways and lawns. Several windows were open, and someone was blasting The Rolling Stones. Near the entrance to the cluster of houses, a rectangular sign made of cast iron hung from a lintel supported by two heavy wooden posts. The sign read, *Sanctuary for Creative Minds*. The line of text at the bottom said, "All for art and art for all." Ava and I looked at each other in the twilight.

"Is this place ...?" mused Ava.

"... a commune?" I finished. I felt our list of suspects multiply.

We walked toward Teddy's police cruiser. The middle house was marked off in police tape. Several young people were clustered around, answering the police chief's questions. As we drew closer, I could make out Teddy, Meiser, and Keith in the fading light. I suddenly realized that skulking around a murder scene with three armed cops wasn't the best plan we had ever had. It was too late, anyway. Meiser had turned and was squinting through the darkness in our direction.

"Jolie? Ava? Is that you?" he asked.

Teddy spun around too, his eyebrows furrowing. "I can't take my eyes off of you ladies for a second!" he grumped.

Bradley appeared at my elbow, startling me. "Hey, you okay?" He looked concerned. "This whole thing is sickening." He had his camera slung around his neck and his voice recorder in his hand. He was in reporter mode.

"I'm okay. Are you?" I asked.

"Yeah, they called me down to the station and took my statement. I thought if I could get a story out, someone might know something, it might help the case." Bradley ran the online edition of *The Village Herald*.

"Well, have you found anything out?" I asked.

"One of her housemates, a girl named Linzie, found her in the kitchen and called the police. The housemate's alibi checks out, she was in her room live streaming on her vlog when the murder took place. Keith already checked the time stamp on the vlog post. But Ava, Jolie. You'll never guess what I found out." Bradley's eyebrows were high on his forehead.

"What?" demanded Ava.

"You know how you told me that they all knew each other even though they pretended like they didn't? The truth is even crazier than that!" he exclaimed.

"What, they are all cousins?" I asked sarcastically.

"No! They all live together. Here! And so does Alyssa's boyfriend, Tad. They are all members of this commune, every last one of them."

"Wow, and they didn't say a word," muttered Ava.

My mind was racing. Well that certainly added some elements to the mystery. Roommates!

"Has anyone said anything about that mask? The one Tad and the killer were both wearing?" I asked while nodding at Ava.

"Mick, Keith, and Teddy are definitely looking for it." Bradley looked over his shoulder and then leaned in conspiratorially. "They got a search warrant for the house proper and went room by room. Now they are trying to get a warrant for the whole commune."

"That's another thing," broke in Ava. "A commune? I didn't think those things existed anymore."

"There are a few here and there," said Bradley. "I'm not sure how this one is set up, but I am guessing that by the end of this investigation, there will be no stone left unturned. I talked to one of the students that live in one of the other houses. She said that it is supposed to be a democracy, but it is actually run by some guy named Quinn." I made a mental note of that name. "Maybe that's why no one said anything. Do you think they subconsciously feel shame for belonging to what some would consider to be weird and kind of . . . cult-y?"

"Good point," Ava said, arching her eyebrows

at me.

"Yeah, but an art cult?" I asked incredulously.

We had been slowly making our way down the driveway during this conversation and finally reached Meiser and Teddy. It was nearly dark, so it was easy to avoid eye contact while hiding my burning cheeks. Suddenly, Meiser grabbed my upper arm and led me a few paces away from the group. I didn't appreciate that he felt like he could steer me like an abandoned bicycle, although his touch did feel like flame against my skin.

"What?" I demanded.

"No, what, you!" he retorted. "Why are you here? This is police business."

"Couple things. First, the murder happened in my class. I watched it. So, I am personally involved. Second, Ava is a licensed private investigator, and I am a part of her ... investigative ... service ... company ..." I was flailing again. I wasn't sure what I was, exactly. It had all made sense when Ava had explained it.

"Hmmm," rumbled Meiser in his deep gravelly voice. "Couple things. First, if and ONLY IF local law enforcement requests help from a licensed PI, they may participate in a criminal investigation, and we have not. Second, your friend may be a licensed PI, but *you* are not. Although you are, as your company name indicates, wonderfully 'bounty-full.'"

My face flushed full-on crimson at the realization that he had been checking up on me, and that his inquiries had yielded the ludicrous company name that Ava had come up with.

"Hey," I shot back. "I have solved multiple murders over the past couple of years!"

"Solved by almost getting yourself maimed or killed, over and over again!" retorted Meiser. "You're a tough girl to love, you know that? You seem determined to live dangerously."

I gasped. *Tough girl to ... love?*

"Please, Jolie," he groaned wearily, "just go home. Go home and be safe. Teddy and I will catch whoever did this. I don't need to worry about some masked commune killer and keep an eye out for you at the same time."

My anger flared up. Typical. Maybe I should just sit this one out. See how long it took them to solve it without Ava and me helping. But no, I owed it to Darla's memory to catch whoever was responsible.

"Hey, did you know that Teddy called me in to the station tonight to make a statement about the murder?"

He stared at me. "Of course I knew. I'm on the case. I was at the station when he called. Your name is on a list of people we want to get statements from. No one understood why you didn't call it in. I told him he should give you both the benefit of the doubt even though by law, we shouldn't have." He gave me a "What's your point?" look.

I ignored that last bit and said, "Is your phone broken? Did you lose my number? Why didn't you just call me?"

Meiser's face fell. He looked wistful for second and mumbled something about being busy right then.

"Well," I said impishly, "you can't stop me from walking around and asking questions. So, I guess we'll see who gets to the truth first. And I won't have the advantage of a huge database and search warrants."

Meiser ground his teeth for a moment. I could tell I had gotten to him. Then he laughed.

"Don't ever stop being you, okay?"

"That seems easy enough," I replied. Nothing had changed. Here we were, repeating the same lines we always repeated. Teasing, insulting, avoiding, using witty retorts to cover hurt and confusion.

"Mick?" I said suddenly.

"Yes, Jolie?"

"You owe me a conversation."

"What?"

"I was in the Dominican Republic. We were talking on the phone. We agreed we needed to sit down. Have a real conversation. An honest one. Remember?"

"I remember," he murmured.

My heart was thundering in my chest. "Well, I'm waiting." Even in the darkness, his eyes burned into mine, making me think that there was some possibility of a future for us. If we could get through all of the baggage piled between us.

"Two days from now, morning, your place?" He called after me.

I shook my head. I didn't want to deal with a Tucker invasion mid-conversation. "Your place," I yelled back.

"Okay, my place!"

"I'll be there!" I shouted back. I turned and stumbled on shaky legs through the twilight, back toward Ava.

We drove in silence for a mile or two. Both of us were lost in thought. I glanced at my friend.

"Well, you know what we need to do next," sighed Ava. I nodded.

"I Spy Slides," we said in unison. We shook our heads about how in sync we were.

"We have to open the restaurant tomorrow! *So* early!" wailed Ava.

"Oh man!" I moaned. "It's two-thirty a.m.! I am tired but my mind is going a million miles an hour. I need to get some things down on I Spy Slides right now. I can pretty much kiss sleeping tonight goodbye. Let's just power through taking notes tonight and catch up on rest tomorrow."

Ava nodded. "I won't be able to sleep either."

"Let's divide up the day tomorrow so we can each get a nap in," I offered. "I can take the first shift, open to lunch, so you can get a little bit of rest. Then you take the lunch rush and work for a few hours, then Carlos can close. We can meet up and work on I Spy Slides. Does that sound okay?"

"I am not going to say no to that!" Ava paused. "We also need to meet with our cooking students and figure out how to proceed from here."

We got back to my house and settled at the kitchen table. Ava opened her email on her laptop and we used information from the student surveys to create a page for each of the students in our online class. Most of them had a thumbnail on their email with a tiny picture, which sufficed for now.

Poppy was passionate about special effects, particularly makeup and costumes. She followed several Hollywood makeup artists on social media, and had her own blog giving theater makeup tips and posting pictures of her own amazing makeup transformations. I noticed that in several of her pictures, she had the huge silver and onyx ring she wore on her ring finger. As she said herself, a good way to keep her straight with all her costumes. I copy-pasted several pictures from Poppy's blog onto her I Spy Slides page and made a list of the makeup artists that she followed. I wrote down a quotation from her latest post, "It is my life's ambition to have a career in makeup special effects. I am determined to make it happen." I read that quotation out loud to Ava. "She sounds very passionate," I commented. "If she had an opportunity that was threatened, that could be motivation. Plus, she could make herself look like a different person ..."

"Make a note of it. Possible motivation and means," agreed Ava. "Okay, let's look at Lahiri." She flipped through the surveys on her computer desktop. "This says that her family and culture are really important to her. She likes to play guitar and cook." I nodded, making notes on the slide.

"Who's next?" I asked.

"Bea, our recent enrollee," announced Ava. We both smiled, feeling a little silly putting someone like her on our list. But a good PI considers everyone. "Bea has lived in Leavensport her whole life. She is happily married to Earl Seevers. Both are retired. They have had financial issues recently because of the retirement investment scam that Lou was involved in," Ava rattled off.

"See, we were laughing about including her," I pointed out, "but she has motivation. Financial stress. You never know." Ava nodded as I typed.

"Alyssa," Ava said next. "She had already gotten in trouble in our class once. She could have been angry. Why she would have picked Darla, though, I don't know." Ava clicked through the survey. "She wants to go into graphic design. She says she wants to start her own design firm in Las Vegas someday. She is confident that she will do it."

I was typing, trying to catch up with Ava's words. "Wow, Vegas. Big dreams. I bet she will, too. She seems very driven," I mused.

"She mentions her boyfriend Tad on the survey," Ava added. "She says they have been together for two years." She paused. "Are we in agreement that he is the most obvious suspect?"

"Of course he is," I replied. "But how many cases have we solved where the crime was committed by the *most obvious suspect*?"

"Um, zero," conceded Ava. "You're right."

"So, we keep asking questions until we find the truth," I declared.

"Because that is just *what we do!*" crowed Ava. "STILL, write down that currently, he is our main suspect."

"Okay—Mod. She didn't write a whole lot about her likes and dislikes." Ava scanned through her short replies. "Not giving a crap seems to be her 'thing.' Gotta admit, it kinda works for her."

"She didn't write anything that could be useful?" I groaned.

"Um, she says she can only work in a setting where people are nice to one another. She hates it when people get picked on. She always wears this necklace with this locket." Ava pointed at a picture.

"I'll make a note of that," I said thoughtfully

taking a closer look. "I remember seeing it. It looks like a Kanji symbol of some kind. We need to look into it. Also, in class she mentioned that she wants to learn how to cook for cheap, so maybe finances are stressful for her? You never know when something could turn out to be a motivation."

"But none of the people in our class could be the actual murderer," Ava pointed out. "We saw them on the screen as Darla was being murdered. That is the very definition of an alibi."

"Yes, we know that none of them literally killed her," I agreed, "but one of them might have a reason to want her dead and know someone who could get the job done. We have to keep our minds open to that possibility."

I closed my eyes to think. "I'm going to add a slide called 'copycat crime' so we can make notes on the two stabbings—the fake one and the real one."

"Good idea," agreed Ava. "We're stuck in the mindset that the person behind the mask the first time is the same one behind the mask the second time. But criminals create copycat crimes all the time." I was typing notes frantically as she talked. "Basically, anyone who knew about what Tad did could have had the idea to copy him, knowing he would likely get blamed for it. Everyone in our class lives together, so they all knew about it, plus anyone that the people in our class told." I nodded. That was possibly a whole list of people we didn't even know.

"Let's make a list of the similarities and differences," I said. "Oh man! I just had a flashback to fifth grade, Mrs. Pumphery showing us how to draw a Venn diagram. Remember?"

"Mrs. Pumphery was the best! How are Brian

from *Hatchet* and Sam from *My Side of the Mountain* similar?" Ava said in a teachery voice. "How are they different?"

We laughed and I opened a fresh slide. I remembered two circles, but from there I was lost. "Wait, do they overlap?" I started drawing random circles on the slide and moving them around.

"Simmer down! You only need two, one for each murder," corrected Ava. "And make them overlap. Yours looks like a weird snowman. The stuff that is the same goes in the middle."

I clicked around and then turned to Ava for approval. "Did I do a good job, Mrs. Martinez?" I gave her a fake innocent look.

Ava rolled her eyes. "Yes. Very good. Now. Similarities: both occurred on camera, during our class, both female victims, both attackers wore a mask with an upside-down face on it," Ava rattled off. "Ooh!" she yelped. "That reminds me! We need to look online and in Halloween stores for masks like that. We need to know if it was store-bought or home-made—Poppy is really creative. I'll make a note of that."

"That is a really good idea. I'll look after work tomorrow. Okay, more similarities. Both stabbed. Both attackers were tall." I was typing as fast as I could.

"Both attackers were silent. Neither one yelled at or insulted or threatened the victims," Ava mused.

"Okay, differences," I continued. "The fake attack was with a retractable theater prop dagger, the real one was with a dark metal stake of some sort."

"The fake attacker revealed himself in the end,

the real attacker did not," Ava added.

"The fake attack may have been planned with the fake victim, but the real victim was definitely not in on it."

As I looked back over our notes, my eyelids began to droop. "Okay, I changed my mind. I think we have a good start here," I said sleepily. "I am going to go take a nap, okay?"

"Yes indeed, bestie!" teased Ava. "We have a class to teach and two businesses that aren't going to run themselves. Rest up. I'll just let myself out."

I was already headed down the hallway to my room. I turned and looked back at Ava as she was locking my door behind her.

"Ava?"

"What?"

"Promise me we'll solve this before Meiser and Teddy do, okay? Because I just couldn't look him in the eye if he solves it first. Promise me?"

Ava just shook her head. "Girl, you've got it bad." Then she closed the door behind her.

Chapter Five

As planned, I opened up Cast Iron Creations, although I don't remember any of it. I don't even remember driving there, which is a scary thought. I was so tired from the events of that last class, then being called down to the station by Teddy, then sneaking out to the commune, then staying up into the wee hours of the morning starting I Spy Slides with Ava.

Luckily, I've done this all so much, I went into a robotic routine: unlock door, turn off alarm, eyeball the front to be sure everything was clean and ready to go, check behind the counter that coffee cups were stocked, coffee makers ready to start, to-go boxes and cups were filled up, then back to the office for any notes from closing, grab the deposit bag and double-check closing figures and totals (normally Ava's job but I can handle it every so often—she would normally run the deposit to the Community Service Credit Union, but I would do that when she got here before going home to crash), lastly—my favorite part—to the kitchen to make sure everything was clean and in place and prepped for breakfast, and that all the items were available that would be needed for lunch and dinner. Since we lived in a small village, there weren't a ton of places to choose from for eating out. Even so, we closed between seven p.m. and eight p.m. every night, after the dinner rush left.

I went through the motions of making beans, sausages, bacon, eggs, pancakes, and the fried donuts while Mirabelle and Spy greeted the guests, and our part-time help, Magda, took care of the front. I was happy we put together an email to the class, but I wasn't looking forward to having an online meeting with the students tonight to discuss the events that had unfolded—especially knowing that they had lied to us from the get-go. One thing that was for sure, I planned to blatantly ask them why they lied.

Ava came in a bit later looking refreshed from getting sleep. I was extremely jealous. I passed on all the information about the morning to help her prepare for the lunch rush. I had worked extra fast to prep everything for lunch and put several cast iron Mexican chicken casseroles in the oven, made sides of rice and beans, and then finished up by mixing up some fresh salsa and guacamole dip, squeezing some lime and lemon on the top to keep it from browning. That way Ava would not have much to do when it came to cooking.

"Wow, thanks, this all looks delicious!"

"I'll take the deposit to the credit union, then I'm headed home to sleep," I said, running back to the office to grab the deposit and shoving it in my large brown leather tote.

"We're still meeting after and doing the discussion with the kids tonight, right?" Ava asked.

I grinned to myself, they weren't that much younger than us, yet here we are calling them 'kids.'

"That's the plan." I grabbed my keys. I didn't want to stick around here. I needed sleep.

Bea Seevers came trotting in, moving straight towards us as I prepared to leave.

"Good Lord, girls, I just heard the news! I can't believe this happened. How are you two always involved in these things?" Mrs. Seevers' pale blue eyes glinted with anticipation of getting the full scoop.

"Well, I am a licensed PI now," Ava said.

"I'm not sure how that relates to our being 'involved in murders'?" I quirked an eyebrow.

"Someone needs to get some sleep so she isn't so cranky!" Ava hissed.

"Of course, you must be tired," Mrs. Seevers cooed. "Let me just tell you one thing you may not be aware of before you head out."

Bea Seevers was chomping at the bit to tell us some juicy gossip. Ava leaned in with anticipation— my eyes were barely open because my brain and body had little energy left.

"What did you hear?" Ava asked looking at me.

"There's going to be a town meeting soon. No one's set a date yet, but obviously, you girls will know when the date is. We really haven't had one in a while, have we? Long overdue."

My head was starting to hurt, and my shoulders slumped. "Is that it? There's going to be a meeting?"

Ava shook her head in frustration at my mood. I glared back.

"Right, yes, I mean, no dear—that's only part of

it. The meeting is going to be about the holes being dug in the fields that are for sale. People are saying that Nestle has something to do with it. He's looking for something. What do you think it could be?"

Nestle? I wonder if that was connected to him wanting a stake in the gallery with Delilah? With everything else that had gone on, I had totally forgotten that I was supposed to be looking into that too.

"I don't know, but we should look into that," Ava said, elbowing me.

Great, this would make things more difficult for me to keep this from her now.

"I'm sorry, I need to run this to the credit union and then get some sleep. Ava, you'll come to my house after Carlos gets here later, right?"

"I can take that for you," Mrs. Seevers said. She had done some volunteer work for us while Ava and I were in Santo Domingo, and we had always trusted her.

"Thank you!" I said happy to hand it over. "The deposit slip is inside and it's locked. They have the key to open the bag."

"I have to run to the credit union for personal reasons," Ava gave me a meaningful look. "I'll take care of it."

I had grabbed my access card to give to Mrs. Seevers. The credit union knew that we were a tight little community, and everyone helped each other out as needed. They devised keycards with fingerprint accesses. Like a smart phone. The business owners could decide which villagers could help out and add their fingerprints to the access cards. We had added my family, the Seevers, and

Miriam and her mom, Mary, as well as Delilah and Betsy to our cards. This made it possible for them to help out with deposits or grab cash when we were running low.

"Oh, okay," I said, realizing that Mrs. Seevers was now on our suspect list, and I was too tired to think straight.

Mrs. Seevers didn't seem suspicious in the change of plans at all. I gave Bea a hug and whispered that I was sorry for being a grump before I headed home for heavenly sleep.

I was jolted awake by Ava shaking me. "Yo, it's time to review everything and get ready to meet the group about the classes."

"Mmmkay" I mumbled throwing off the covers, sliding into my slippers, and moving downstairs groggily toward the teapot. "Let me get some caffeine. You load the slides."

Truth is, I felt a lot better, but I wasn't used to not sleeping throughout the night and then snoozing in the middle of the day. I shook the cobwebs from my head after having prepared my caffeinated coconut chai tea adding a splash of milk with a little sweetener.

"Hit it," I said taking a large gulp and feeling the burn going down my throat.

"You still look sleepy," Ava noted.

"I am. I'll be fine as soon as I drink this."

"We still have time before we have to be back to meet with the group. Go put some real shoes on," she looked down at my black cat slippers, grinning, "and let's go to Chocolate Capers to do this. Put your tea in a to-go mug so you can wake up on the way there. It will do you good to get some fresh air after sleeping."

"You don't have to ask me twice. I'm always up for a brownie and more tea!" I went to the couch where I had kicked off my Birkenstocks and slipped them back on as we headed for a chocolate treat.

Parking on the street, I admired the red and white awning over Chocolate Capers and No Cones About It. The two shops shared a building but were separated by a wall. Betsy had done a lot of redecorating when her aunt died. She always had some extravagant chocolate item in the window's showcase as customers walked inside. Today, it was a pair of decadent high heels with a yellow flower made with molded fondant. She was an artist with chocolate!

I wasn't expecting to see what I saw when we walked into the shop. Teddy was sitting at a table in the corner with Tabitha and they were in close quarters, discussing something. He looked over at us and seemed embarrassed, then waved as his cheeks turned crimson.

Tabitha gave me a knowing wink. Did that mean they were on a date? She had asked me before if he was seeing anyone. I was weirded out that my therapist was giving me facial cues about her love life.

Heading to the counter, Ava whispered, "What is that about?"

Betsy must have heard because she seemed to be overcompensating with a gleeful tone, "Oh now, ladies, it looks like Teddy has finally found love. And I say, good for him!" She nearly squealed. My heart sank knowing she was in pain.

Ava side-eyed me.

"I doubt that, Betsy. I know she's the town therapist, but you know as well as we do that she helps out on cases from time to time," I said reminding her that Tabitha used to be in the FBI Since Teddy can't afford to hire anyone else full-time after adding Meiser and Keith to the force, he brings Tabitha in on an as-needed basis.

"I agree. No way Teddy is going for that hoe bag!" Ava declared.

"Ava, she isn't a horrible person!" What on earth?

"No need for names there, slugger," Bradley said, walking up and smiling at Betsy with his boyish good looks. "Are you two ordering?"

"Oh yeah, two chocolate brownies and a cup of Perfect Pumpkin spiced tea," I said grabbing my wallet from my tote.

"I'll take a coffee," Ava said.

"Aren't you getting a brownie?" I asked.

Everyone laughed except me.

"You aren't kidding?" Betsy asked.

I shook my head in all seriousness.

"I'll have a brownie, too," Ava rolled her eyes.

"You want the brownies with the chocolate icing, right?" Betsy asked, leaning into the baked goods counter for the ones with the icing.

We both nodded in enthusiasm.

Moving to a small table near the counter, we took our seats and got the computer fired up. I took a sip of my tea and ate my first brownie in two large bites, feeling much better.

"Geesh, why are you hoovering that brownie?"

Ava asked, waiting for the computer to come to life.

"I haven't eaten anything since before class yesterday."

"Why don't you eat while you cook? I do."

My blue eyes bulged out. "Please tell me that is not true, Ava. That's a health issue. You can't do that!"

"I didn't say I used my fingers and picked around in the food that I served. All you have to do is make a little more, or if there are some leftovers, we always eat some!"

"Oh, okay. I left right after my shift today so no leftovers. I was too tired to even think this—"

"SHHHHHHH!" Ava reached for my mouth with her hand.

"Rude!" I slapped her hand away as she pointed to Bradley and Betsy.

I looked over my shoulder, but Ava kicked me under the table. "OW! What is your problem?"

Teddy, Tabitha, Bradley, and Betsy all looked over at us as I rubbed my leg.

"Sorry, we are working out some kinks with our online class. Technology, such a pain," Ava waved her hand. I grudgingly agreed while glaring at her.

"Just listen to Bradley," Ava said through gritted teeth.

"Anyways, I know rumors have been circling around here lately about Lydia. And, yes, we *used* to be an item, but not anymore. I wanted to ask you out. Er-um, would you like to have dinner with me?"

I couldn't see what Bradley was doing because Ava would kick me again, but I could see Ava's face contort and it looked like she smelled something horrible. Bradley must really be nervous.

"Oh, wow. Yes, the rumors are rampant, aren't they? Um, I'm tempted to say yes, but it feels wrong with Lydia pregnant and everything up in the air with who the father is," Betsy stammered.

"Oh, it's not mine. I know this for sure now. I demanded a test. She and I are over. Of course, I want her and the baby to be healthy. Regardless of what's taken place between us, I'd never wish any harm on her or that baby."

While I couldn't see Betsy or Bradley, I could see Teddy ignoring Tabitha and homing in on what was happening at the counter.

"What's going on?" I whispered to Ava when I couldn't hear anything.

"She's thinking," Ava said.

"Um, okay, dinner couldn't hurt," Betsy said. "Thanks for asking." She wrote down her number and handed it to him.

"Whoa, go Bradley!" I said as he walked out the door.

"That was hard to watch," Ava said.

"Yeah, it seemed difficult for Teddy to watch it too," I said, nodding at Teddy, who had a far-off look on his face.

Ava turned to look at him and I kicked her hard under the table. "WHAT THE?"

"Ladies, here's a pot of tea on the house. And Ava, I brought you another brownie to make it even." Betsy laid our goodies on the table.

"So, when's the big date?" Ava asked, forgetting about my payback.

Betsy did her high-pitched giggle that sounded like a gleeful child's laugh. She was adorable in every way. "I don't know. I hope soon. I haven't been on a date in so long."

"Yeah, well, Teddy didn't look too thrilled about what he saw," I said, getting in on the gossip.

"Really?" Betsy asked half-turning to try and catch a glimpse of Teddy, who was looking at her.

"He looked devastated to me."

"Whatever, his loss," Ava said, taking a big bite of brownie.

Betsy moved back behind the counter to wait on a customer that had just walked in.

"Do you think we should start an I Spy Slides for the entire Nestle thing?" Ava asked.

Yes, yes, I did. "Mrs. Seevers was just telling us what she heard. I say we focus on Darla's murder. We have enough on our plates right now. We may change our minds after the town meeting, though."

"What the heck is going on out there?" I pointed across the street to Costello's Grocery Store that was catty-corner to Chocolate Capers. Lydia held two bags of groceries in one arm while using the other to point angrily at Nestle. I noticed Teddy and Tabitha looking as well.

"What on earth could those two be arguing about?" Ava asked.

"No clue," I said as Nestle grabbed Lydia's free arm and began to pull her.

I saw Teddy and Tabitha jump up and move to the door.

Lydia broke free but a sack of groceries fell to the sidewalk. Teddy jogged across the street with Tabitha following as Nestle took off around the corner of the store.

"Whoa, Lydia looks ticked." I said. "Maybe we

should go help?"

"Nah, they've got it under control," Ava said, pouring me another cup of tea.

Good point.

Chapter Six

We were getting ready to meet our students to discuss the events that took place the night before and to determine if we would continue with the course next week or refund their money. Bradley wasn't here since it wasn't a planned class event, plus this shouldn't take too long.

"So, you'll take the lead, right?" Ava asked.

"Yep, you are going to hit the record button on the class when we start this time, right?"

"Got it ready to go."

"Hey, everyone. So, I know you all have been informed of what's going on especially since you all know each other." I crossed my arms like the scolding teacher. So much for taking a soft approach then asking them why they lied to us.

"I don't understand why you all lied," Ava blurted out.

I noticed none of them were looking at the camera. Mod was wringing her hands in anxiety. Alyssa had her arms crossed and was rocking on her heels. Poppy was rubbing the back of her neck like she was nervous, and Lahiri seemed alert and jumpy.

"Listen, what happened to Darla was horrible. I am still having a hard time believing all this. Now, we find out you all know each other. I can't imagine how you all are handling it."

Mod, who seemed to not care about much, began to sob, then rushed away from the camera.

Alyssa was the first one to speak. "We all want to apologize to you both. We've known each other since we were in an art history course together and got grouped together on a project. We hit it off so well—" Alyssa's eyes filled to the brim with tears as she gulped trying to gain her composure. She was shaking all over like she was freezing.

I felt like a jerk for giving them such a hard time right off the bat. But, they had been lying to us since the get-go. Ava and I had agreed we weren't going to tell them we knew since before Darla's murder. We figured we might be able to use Peggy's Pies and Purses as a place to do some undercover work.

"Sorry, we are all majoring in some type of the arts. We wanted to see if we could take your course and use some tricks of our majors to create an illusion. None of us knew this would—"

"Hello? You cut out." The computer screen on our end went black then a bright blue squiggly line began pulsating through the middle of the screen. I looked at Ava wishing we would have thought to ask Bradley to be here.

Ava hit the computer. Nothing.

The screen began to flip, and I thought we would see the students again, but an odd figure appeared. Someone in the upside-down face mask came into view with a black background. The person had on a white long-sleeved shirt with black horizontal stripes. A distorted voice said, "Your friend, Darla, will not be the last to suffer the fate of Picasso's Peril. Art is a lie that makes us realize the truth."

The screen went back to normal. By the look on the students' faces, they had all seen the same thing on their screens too. Mod was back at that point and looked like she was in shock.

"Are you all there together?" I asked.

"Yes," Lahiri answered.

"Well, not me," Mrs. Seevers spoke up. I nodded at her.

"Did you all see and hear that?"

Many nodded in agreement, with a look of shock Poppy, looking like a punk rocker confirmed verbally in a deep voice—it seemed she was good at altering her speech too.

"I don't know. This class has been chaotic from night one. Originally, I called us together to take a vote as to whether we should continue or refund the money. But I'm thinking it is pretty clear that we should cancel the course and do a refund," I said looking at Ava who looked as panic-stricken as I did in that moment.

"I agree with what you originally said," Poppy spoke up. "We should vote. I am really enjoying the class other than—well—what happened last night."

My phone rang. It was Meiser. "Hold on a second," I said into the phone, then asked Ava to take over for the time being.

"What's up?" I said.

"Ava texted something happened on the

computer?"

"Oh, I didn't know she did that." I told him about meeting the students to discuss if we should continue or not and then how it was hacked by someone wearing the same mask as the killer was.

"I know I asked you to stay out of it, but we all met this morning and agreed that you and Ava have a unique in with this group. Will you see if they are willing to move forward with the course?"

"I can try. I just made a big spiel about refunding and canceling right before you called. Was everyone on the team in agreement we help with the investigation?"

"Yes, Teddy pulled Tabitha in on this because part of what she did in the past was cybercrimes. Now, with this new hack from what could be the killer, she will be extremely useful. She'll want to add some things to your computer and possibly be there for your classes."

Maybe that is what Teddy and Tabitha were discussing today at Chocolate Capers.

"Okay, let me see what I can do." I got off the phone with Mick and made a quick call to my friend Peggy in Tri-City since she had told us that her shop was located near the college campus.

"Hey woman, what's happening in that teensy town of yours?" Peggy was way hipper than I could ever hope to be.

"You wouldn't believe me if I told you! So much since we last met! I don't have a lot of time, but I'll call back and fill you in later. We need to set up another meeting with you and Gemma ASAP!"

"Of course. Why?"

"I know she is a wiz at marketing, but what

about technology?"

"Boy, someone has a good memory! Yes, I believe I briefly mentioned that last November about her tech skills."

"We need to catch up on what all has gone down this last week. For now, let's schedule a time to meet—Ava and I will come to you."

After setting something up with the gals from Tri-City, I went back in to find Ava telling the students that none of them better have that stupid mask and there had better be no more pranks in the future.

"Whoa, what's going on?" I asked.

Mod seemed to be in meltdown mode and Alyssa had moved to wherever Mod was and was consoling her.

Lahiri spoke up first, "Miss Ava thinks we may have created another prank. I swear we don't have that sick of humor. We did not do that nor do we know who it was."

"How are we supposed to know what is and isn't true anymore?" Ava argued.

"Now, girls, I think we can give these young ladies a break. They've just lost their friend."

"Are you all in the same room?" I asked, again noting Alyssa was with Mod.

"We are now," Alyssa said of her and Mod. "There are large houses on the property. We all share houses. Each house has two kitchens. Mod and I stay in this house but for the purposes of your class, we were using the different kitchens. I heard her crying and came to be with her."

Alyssa put an arm around Mod, who finally spoke up, "I think—" more sobs, long silence— "we should keep going. It's horrible wh-wha-what happened. This is a way to honor Darla."

"I agree," Lahiri said. "Let's continue the course."

Alyssa, Poppy, and Mrs. Seevers were all bobbing their heads in accord.

Well, that was easy enough. "Okay, it's settled, we'll meet back at our scheduled time. But, no more lies. Also, Ava and I would like to meet with you all face-to-face to shed some light on this."

"We can work that out," Alyssa said.

"We'll be in touch," I said, and ended the session.

"Did you get all that?"

"Yep," Ava hit stop on the recorder on the computer.

"Good thinking, texting Meiser," I said. "I called Peggy. We are going to meet her and Gemma again about what's going on. I have an idea of how they may be able to help us from Tri-City. Meantime, Meiser said Teddy has Tabitha working on the case. She may add something to my computer and be at some of our classes moving forward."

"Yikes, there's going to be a huge team working together on this," Ava said.

"Well, the suspect pool has dramatically increased. We have an entire group of commune members to investigate."

Meiser and I had set up to have our talk at his house this morning. He had wanted to meet at my place, but since I never knew for sure who would burst in at any given moment, I thought better of that.

I took a deep breath and knocked on his door. I saw Lucky Lou pop his orange and white face out from the curtain in the front window then Stewart, Mick's one-eyed kitty, bounced up next to Lucky.

Mick opened the door wearing worn blue jeans, sweat socks, and a tight-fitted chocolate brown V-neck T-shirt that made his large brown eyes pop.

"Hey," I said, brushing by him and taking a seat at his dining room table where I saw he had some tea and chocolate chip cookies sitting out. "I see these two have become fast buddies."

Stewart and Lucky both came up to me for a neck rub.

"They've missed seeing you," he said.

I poured some tea from the Japanese tea pot I had bought him as a gift. It was supposed to be a joke. He liked to pick on me back when we were getting along well and starting a relationship about how much tea I drank. He said he needed to get a kettle. So, I bought him a kettle, and what I thought was a beautiful Japanese tea set. "I see you put this to good use."

"Actually, I use it almost every day."

"What was with all the teasing about my tea addiction?"

"I've always preferred coffee, but having tea made me think of you and feel you were close to me."

"Right. Before we go there—"

"Go where?" He asked.

"Back to what we do. Flirt, suggest, hint. Why don't we have the difficult conversation first?"

Meiser tilted his head, tracing his finger around the rim of the teacup in thought. "Okay."

"You said we needed to talk when I was in the Dominican Republic. I came back ready. I saw you taking Lydia to a doctor's appointment. I do what I do. I went inward. You tried to contact me, but I needed time. What I did wrong was that I didn't tell you that I needed that time. I should have. That was wrong." I blurted it all out quickly in one breath and then waited.

Then, I waited more while he took his hands and ran them through his thick brown locks.

"Well?" I asked.

"Well, what?"

"Your turn."

"I know. My reaction was to take off."

More waiting. "That's it?"

"Yes."

"Manswer!"

"What does that even mean?"

"It means a short, curt answer that isn't really an answer. You didn't just leave. You took an undercover job. You set it all up. You never told me anything. You were just gone from the face of the earth."

"Jolie, I never told you anything because you weren't talking to me."

"You're doing it again! Manswer! No, I wasn't talking to you. I told you I was wrong. You could have left a message on my machine. You could have texted or emailed. You could have come into the restaurant and just blurted it out at my face!"

Meiser stared at me a moment before giving in

to a huge grin. "'Blurted it out at my face!'" he mocked me.

We both laughed, "Well, you know what I meant."

"I do know. I'm sorry. I was hurt and angry. What is wrong with us?"

I bit my bottom lip. "Is the baby yours?"

"No."

"How do you know for sure?"

"I know because I never slept with Lydia."He looked me square in the eyes, not blinking. I was sure he was telling the truth.

"How did you two get so close while I was gone?" So, if Mick and Bradley were not the father of the baby—that only left Keith!

"I had a flare-up with the MS. I went to the hospital and she was my nurse. She had just found out she was pregnant. She didn't know who the father was. She helped me with my flare-up and I listened to her. You know, she doesn't hate you as much as you think she does."

"Really? What makes you say that?"

"A lot of what we talked about was you."

"That had to be an interesting conversation."

"I talked about you a lot—about us. Maybe I was being a jerk. I knew you two had issues, so maybe a part of me was trying to punish you by talking to her. She's had a tumultuous family life too. But I swear, we never did anything more than talk. She helped me with my MS flare-up and I listened. I don't think she has any friends."

"She and Betsy are best friends," I said.

"Not since Betsy took over her aunt's business

and left nursing," he said.

I had no idea, but now that I thought about it, I hadn't seen them together. "So, it doesn't bother you that she lied to the entire town saying that you could be the father? That she threw it in my face? That feels like hatred to me."

"Of course that bothers me. I addressed that with her. She was embarrassed. You rub her the wrong way. She sees you as having the life she wished she could have had. Your family makes you insane, but she wishes she had a family that cared that much about her and this baby."

"It sounds like you're justifying things for her."

"I'm sure it sounds like that to you. Your feelings are valid. I don't know a better way to explain it. I get why you are upset. I also get why she feels the way she feels. Maybe you two are like oil and water and it will always be this way."

"Maybe. Well, okay, I guess that's answered for now. I was ready last Thanksgiving. Then, you pulled the rug out from under my feet."

"My family put you in danger. I still don't know what's going on with them. I'm still worried about that."

"There's always something. Your family, my family, Lydia, our age difference, your MS, my stubbornness—and I'd wager there will always be something. Nothing seems to be easy with us."

"How are you ten years younger than me and so smart?"

"Therapy."

"Noted," he laughed.

"Maybe we should do therapy together?"

Mick coughed up the cookie he just bit into. "I

know Tabitha."

"Me too."

"I work with her. That is a conflict of interest."

"Okay," I grabbed a cookie and bit into it. "Good!"

"It's your recipe. I got a cast-iron cookie sheet. I'll admit to having to make many batches. I kept burning them because I kept forgetting how cast iron holds the heat."

"Well, this batch is perfect."

"Underdone, the way you like them." He smiled at me.

My phone vibrated and I saw that Ava was texting.

"Who's that?"

"Ava, she wants me to meet her and Delilah at the restaurant for some meeting."

Meiser's phone rang.

"Looks like duty calls," he said.

"I guess we'll have to finish this later." I scratched the kitties' head and moved to the door. Mick reached for me and kissed me, like it was the most natural thing in the world.

I drifted out the door on a cloud.

Oh boy, that feeling I thought I had lost. It was back.

Chapter Seven

I parked and then hustled in the front door of the restaurant, smiling at Mirabelle and Spy on the way in. I loved coming in the front of Cast Iron Creations. I loved to imagine what it must be like as a customer. The sun was shining through the front windows, everything was neat and clean and bustling with happy customers eating tasty food.

The dining room smelled amazing. The tea and cookies that Meiser had served me at his house were delicious—almost as delicious as that kiss—but had not filled me up, and the thought of a real meal made my stomach rumble. The specials sign said "Mexican Polenta Bowl" and the side dish was listed as Spicy Skillet Peaches. Carlos had been working his magic again!

Ava and Delilah sat at a four-top in the corner. As soon as I saw Delilah, my chest felt a little tight. I had agreed to keep Delilah's secret about Nestle owning a share in her gallery but wasn't comfortable keeping something from Ava. I concentrated hard on keeping a casual expression as I sauntered over to the table.

"What's wrong with your face?" Ava demanded immediately. "You look like you do when you have a wedgie."

I was really bad at this. I managed to roll my eyes and sit down. I snuck a look at Delilah, but she was looking at Ava. At that moment, Magda showed up at our table to take our order. Her hair had grown out a bit and she had shaved it off on one side since the last time I had worked with her. The long side swept over her forehead, creating a bold contrast to the shaved side. She could pull off the coolest looks.

"Are you guys hungry or just hanging out?" she asked, smiling.

"I want whatever I smell," I announced.

"That would be the polenta bowl," replied Magda. "It is selling like crazy. I had it on my lunch break and it is out of this world. Beans, fresh veggies, and cilantro on top with some avocado. Mmm! And definitely get the skillet peaches with it. They are sweet and spicy at the same time."

My jaw dropped and my stomach growled even more. "We should give you a sales bonus if you do that routine at every table. Wow!"

"Yeah, seriously." Delilah nodded. "I wasn't planning on eating but now I want the same thing."

"Make that three!" added Ava.

"Wise choices," grinned Magda. "I'll be back with waters in a second."

I found myself looking out of the windows to keep myself from looking at Ava and Delilah. I could keep my guilt under control if I was around each separately, but together was too much. I resolved to find out what Nestle was up to as soon as possible. Madga dropped off three glasses of water and a pitcher of more ice water. I smiled thanks and took a sip, then turned back to the window.

Lydia drove past in her car. It was just a split-second sighting, but just enough to get me thinking about her. Meiser had said that she didn't hate me as much as I thought. That she didn't have any friends. I felt a weird pang.

But ... she had told basically the entire town that she had slept with my on-again-off-again boyfriend. That was clearly intended to hurt me specifically. Although I know better than anyone that being in pain makes you act out in ways you normally wouldn't. I shook my head. I was staring out the window to try to clear my head, not make it even more muddled.

"Earth to Jolie," said Delilah.

"Oh, sorry, I didn't mean to ignore you guys," I apologized. "I think my brain is still foggy from our all-nighter."

"Duly noted," Ava said. "Try to keep up because this is important PI intel."

Suddenly, I was all ears. "What did you find out?"

Ava waggled her eyebrows. "Well, it is more of an idea. We want to know more about the members of the art commune, right?"

"Yeah, that would be great!"

"We were thinking ... if only we had someone who knew a lot about art ... who could maybe pass as an art student ... who was interested in joining the Sanctuary for Creative Minds ..." Ava had a pretend contemplative look on her face.

"Oh wow! That would be ideal!" I practically

yelled.

"Jolie," declared Ava, "I would like you to meet Dee, former business major, who is switching to a fine arts painting major at Triopolis University." Delilah beamed at me.

I gasped and looked at Ava, who nodded. "She's willing to go undercover and try to find out as much as she can about those art students."

Magda arrived with a huge tray and began distributing the steaming dishes to the three of us. We abruptly abandoned our discussion of the plan to dig into the delicious food. Both dishes were immaculately seasoned, the flavors perfectly balanced. Carlos had a gift. I wondered for a moment if Carlos' loyalty to us was holding him back. Maybe he belonged in his own restaurant in some big city, drinking in fame and making a mint. But that was a train of thought for another day. Between the murder and Nestle and Meiser and Lydia, I have enough on my plate right now.

"I have my whole backstory completely planned out," said Delilah, when we all came up for air from devouring the incredible food. "Childhood, education, hobbies, interests ... I even have the beginnings of a portfolio of paintings that I could be working on. 'Dee' is really into Surrealism."

"I'm so lucky that my lovely lady is so darn talented," said Ava, gazing in adoration at Delilah.

I smiled. Those two were such a good couple. And they had been through so much together. At the same time, though, a part of me was cringing as I watched Ava flirt with her girlfriend because I knew Delilah wasn't being totally honest. And I was helping her. But Delilah was taking time out of her busy life, and putting herself in harm's way to help us out—again! Now I felt like I somehow owed both of them a debt of guilt they didn't even know about.

I sighed. Tabitha was going to get an earful next session.

One way to make myself feel better, I knew for sure, was to make some headway on the mystery of why Nestle was so interested in owning a piece of Delilah's family's property. I couldn't prove it, but I was sure he was involved in organized crime.

Ava's family knew what it was like to be pressured by the mafia. I suddenly had a flashback to the many times I had enjoyed hanging out in the Martinezes' beautiful, cozy kitchen in the Dominican Republic with that delightful family. What would Thiago, Ava's dad, do in this situation?

In my mind, I imagined all of the mafias in the world as spiderwebs, stretched across their various areas of influence, all trying to draw people into their net, where they could keep them trapped and controlled. I thought of Meiser yanking himself free from the Sicilian mafia and all that it had cost him. I wondered how many delicate silver strands had stretched into Leavensport. And if so, which spiders had spun them, and what did they want?

I shook myself. My mind was wandering to strange places for sure. I looked around. Ava and Delilah hadn't seemed to notice, both shoveling the last few bites of the exquisite meal into their mouths and talking over the details of the plan.

"She's going to go over to the commune sometime in the next few days," Ava was explaining. "Gemma knows someone in the registration office at the college who will make her a student ID. You know, just in case."

Delilah nodded. "I'll start by just talking to

people. I wouldn't mind flying under the radar for a few days, picking up some information before whoever is in charge knows I'm there. I have a portfolio, some clothes packed in a suitcase, and my art supplies bag that I used in college."

"Wow." I was in awe. It was a really good plan.

"We are thinking that if she acts like she has nowhere to stay, eventually someone might let her crash on their couch," Ava said excitedly. "Then she could really snoop!"

"We sure owe you one for this," I said, smiling at Delilah. She gave me an odd smile back. Was she doing this out of guilt?

I grabbed the check out of Magda's hand and paid for everyone's meal. Maybe I had some guilt issues, too.

We parted ways after we ate. Ava and Delilah declared they were going to Ava's place to watch a movie and finish the details of their plan.

I waved goodbye and walked down the sidewalk toward my car. Suddenly, Aunt Fern appeared in my path.

"Aunt Fern! How are you?"

"Jolie, dear, I'm just fine. I was actually coming to see you." She patted my shoulder. I noticed she had new earrings dangling from her ears. *Interesting.* "Do you still have any of that perfume I got you for Christmas?" she asked.

"Yes, but it's at my house," I replied. "Why?"

"Can I come by tonight and spritz some on myself? I used all of my perfume and I've got a date. A blind date! I finally get to find out who has been sending me gifts and things. Whoever he is, he left these earrings in my mailbox," she tilted one ear toward me, "with a note and his phone number. We've been texting. We're going to meet at M&M for dinner." Aunt Fern blushed pink and grinned.

"You know, Aunt Fern, if you have his phone number, you can find out who is texting you."

"Oh, Jolie," she rolled her eyes at me. "You don't know the first thing about romance. The mystery is what makes it tantalizing!"

I almost warned her to be careful, but I was fairly certain the man she was meeting was our mayor, who had purchased those earrings at Gemma's shop just a few days ago. I kept my mouth shut, but smiled to myself.

I went to my car and drove around and found myself heading toward the outskirts of town. I went over to the land that was for sale and parked.

I remembered being so sleepy as I rode in the car to the airport with Ava, on the way to solve a mystery in Santo Domingo. I was sure I had seen someone digging a hole in one of the fields that were for sale. So many things had happened at the time to pull my mind away from that image, but I was there now, looking at the field where the figure had been. I got out and walked through the tall grass.

Now, in broad daylight, it seemed less ominous. The "phantom" was likely a prankster, a vandal, a hobbyist with a metal detector, looking for old coins. A fresh breeze blew. I walked slowly through the field, enjoying nature. A startled rabbit bounced away from me. A fly buzzed near my ear.

I crisscrossed the field, and eventually came across the spot that had been dug up. It was several weeks old, but there was evidence of about twelve holes dug in a cluster of maybe fifteen feet square.

Rain and time had filled most of the holes in, but judging from the size of the dirt piles beside them, none of the holes were terribly deep. Whoever had been digging had known that what they were looking for was buried close to the surface. Interesting.

My detective senses sprang to life. I scanned the surrounding vegetation. There was no path of crushed grass and plants, no ruts gashed in the earth leading away, so no large truck or equipment had been brought in. Chances were, whoever had dug here had NOT found what they were looking for.

Maybe I would invest in a metal detector myself.

Bea had said people were connecting Nestle to all of this. What could be buried in a field in the outskirts of the tiny village of Leavensport that could interest someone like Nestle? He seemed to have his hand in everything. And he was always so cool and confident, like he knew something everyone else didn't.

Secrets and lies, that's how the mafia functioned. Secrets and lies and power and pressure. Making good people do things they didn't want to do so they could make money or get power or stay out of prison. It was disgusting. That feeling had been creeping into our village. That sense of things done behind the scenes, of people being pressured to act or to not act.

I wished Meiser wasn't so vehement in his refusal to discuss his knowledge of organized crime with me. There was so much I wanted to know. I would give anything to find out for sure if Nestle was involved in the Italian Mafia, like Mick and his family, or some other mafia. If he would answer one simple question, I would know if I was barking up the wrong tree or not. But it didn't seem like that was how our relationship worked. So, I would figure it out on my own.

The breeze lifted my curly hair off of my neck. A monarch butterfly settled on a flower nearby. Suddenly, I felt angry and defensive. *This is my village, my people. No one will use us for whatever corrupt purpose they have planned.* I nodded fiercely at the butterfly, and marched back toward my car.

On the way, I saw a piece of paper caught in the grass. It was a receipt from Costello's Grocery Store for the purchase of "unisex sunglasses, black, $12.99." Of course, the wind could have blown it there from far away, or out of someone's car window. I noticed curly writing in black pen on the back. "Skip class or camera off so one can see." *What on earth did that mean?* I tucked it in my pocket.

My afternoon walk infused me with vigor. I came home and wrote out lesson plans for our next online class—introducing how to cook the perfect steak. I planned out the menu for the next week at Cast Iron Creations, sending a few text messages to Carlos asking for his input. I looked through my folder of written notes on the murder case to see if anything new jumped out at me. Teddy still had my laptop, and Ava had hers at her house, so I would have to organize my secret investigation on Nestle the old-fashioned way.

I dug through my drawers until I found an old spiral-bound notebook to use as my secret file on Nestle. It had a dark blue cover with a puffy cat sticker on it. I needed to keep it separate from the I Spy Slides I worked with Ava on, for obvious reasons. Everything about this seemed wrong, but I doubted that betraying Delilah's trust by telling Ava what had happened would make me feel any better or do anyone any good. I was stuck between a rock and a hard place, and the only means of escape was solving the mystery.

The sun was beginning to set as I made myself two eggs over-easy and a piece of toast. I settled onto the couch with a book as I ate. Tabitha always reminded me to take care of myself, to allow myself to step away from my responsibilities to rejuvenate myself. She seemed to sense how difficult it was for me to do.

Considering the sweat and mud that had accumulated on my body from the adventures of the day, a hot bath seemed in order. I filled the tub, adding salts and aromatic oil. I turned on some nature sounds on my phone and lit some scented candles.

I was about to climb in when I heard a knock on the door. *Aunt Fern! I forgot!* I wrapped myself in a towel and answered the door.

"Oh, Jolie, you should never come to the door like that!" Aunt Fern chided, walking past me and into my bathroom. "What if I had been a murderer? Or worse, Mick? What would he think of you?" I covered my mouth with my hand to keep from chuckling. Wait until I tell Meiser that he outranked a murderer in terms of the worst person to appear at my door. I heard her rustling around in my bathroom closet. "Here it is," she said. She reappeared, sniffing her own wrist rapturously. "Thanks, dear! Now, it looks like you have a relaxing evening planned for yourself. I'll let you get back to it."

"Well, text me and tell me how your date

goes—." I waved at her retreating back.

"Sure, kid, but don't wait up!" she purred, gliding out the door. The second it closed, I cracked up. She was something else. I walked back into the bathroom and climbed into the tub. Still blazing hot, very relaxing. My muscles unclenched. *Ahhhh.* I had been reading the book Tabitha gave me and I was now over halfway done with it. I loved reading in the tub.

My phone buzzed. Ava, sending a picture of "Dee" in her "undergraduate art major" disguise. I laughed quietly. My phone buzzed again. Meiser.

It was wonderful seeing you today.

Thanks, I texted back. *It was good to see you, too. We had a real conversation, finally.*

Finally, he replied. *Nice.*

Well? We have a bad habit of avoiding talking about what is important.

Yeah, we are a lot better at just flirting and kissing. I was already rosy from the bath, but this comment made me flush even more.

It has gotten us by so far, I suppose, I admitted.

It has been pretty fun, he agreed. *Did I interrupt bedtime?*

No, just taking a bath. I got a little muddy today. I sent the message and then yelped, realizing how it sounded.

A bath, you say? Oh crap.

Yes.

Do you need help washing your back? I can be there in five minutes.

Shut up, Mick.

Yes, ma'am. I giggled and flushed even more.

Good night, Meiser.

Good night, Jolie.

I had been home for barely an hour after work the next day. I had fed the cats and was flipping through the channels when my cell vibrated on the coffee table.

Can I come over? asked Ava.

Of course! I typed. Less than a minute later, my front door opened.

"What's up?" I asked.

Ava shook her head and wandered over to the counter, filling my kettle at the sink and putting it on the stove. She pulled out two mugs and two tea bags from the tin on the shelf. Why wasn't she answering me?

I stood up and walked over to my friend, putting my hand on her arm. Her shoulders slumped.

"Delilah decided to start her undercover investigation today," Ava said. "She just drove over to the commune."

"That's great!" I replied. "What's wrong?" I went over to the table and pulled out a chair for her. She absentmindedly walked over and sat on it. I joined her.

"She was so excited to do it," Ava whispered. "And it seemed like such a good idea while we were planning, but now that she's over there, all I can think about is the fact that I sent the woman that I love to a house where a murder took place and the killer is still at large, possibly even *living at that very house!*"

"Delilah can handle it," I reassured her.

"Remember Santo Domingo?" Delilah had rescued us from being held captive by kidnappers. She was a force to be reckoned with.

Ava nodded but still looked worried. The kettle whistled, and I hopped up and filled both of the mugs. I stirred in milk and sugar and brought both mugs to the table.

"I think I just need something else to think about to keep my mind off of it."

"Hey!" I said. "Meiser and I have been talking a little." Normally I am not one to offer up such an emotionally sensitive topic, but my best friend needed something to distract her from her worries.

"Oh really!" Ava's eyebrows shot up and a half-smile bloomed on her face. A juicy story on someone's love life is the best antidote for anxiety. I decided to play up the drama.

"Yeah, girl. I went over to his house!" She was leaning in to hear all the details. "We hung out alone together for a really long time. We talked and talked."

"Yeah? Did you do anything else?"

"Oh, baby, did we. He gave me the most wonderful—" I stopped abruptly to take a loud slurp from my mug.

"The most wonderful what?" Ava demanded. I grinned.

"—the most wonderful cup of tea!" I cackled.

"WHAT?" Ava looked ready to blow a gasket.

I sat up straight and laced my fingers together on the tabletop. I looked at her primly. "Yes. It was very flavorful."

Ava rolled her eyes. "You're the absolute worst, you know that?"

I sighed. "Sorry. We did kiss, though."

"There it is!" Ava hooted triumphantly. "I knew it!"

"I don't know what to think," I said, dropping the act. "It seems like we really care about each other. We just have so much to work through if we are going to be a functional couple, though."

"What about that whole mess with Lydia?"

"According to him, she's making it up. They were never together. I believe him. And you know what that means? Keith is the only one left who can be the baby daddy!"

"If that is true, Lydia has more issues than we thought. Why on earth would anyone sleep with Keith?"

"Hey, we all have done things to other people that we shouldn't have." I shrugged and grinned at her. We both knew Keith and I were once an item. At that moment, I heard Ava's phone chime.

"I never thought I'd hear you take her side," she commented, digging her phone out of her pocket. "Hey, it's Delilah!" She read the message and her face changed. She passed the phone to me.

Going even better than expected. Already made friends with two of them. Told them I don't have anywhere to stay so they are letting me crash on their couch tonight. Love you, sweetie! Don't text back, you'll blow my cover. Love, Dee

Chapter Eight

I had almost insisted that Ava take the day off today because she was so distraught about Delilah being incommunicado since last night. But I realized that sitting at home with nothing to do makes anxiety ten times worse. I didn't want her pacing a hole in her carpet.

I peeked up into the front. Instead, she was pacing a hole in the tile behind the register. I didn't worry about her strange behavior scaring off the customers. The people of Leavensport had witnessed enough of our erratic displays over the years, nothing fazed them. In Delilah's defense, we hadn't exactly planned out how long she would be gone when she went undercover, and how we could communicate. We were just kind of flying by the seat of our pants with this.

Lunch was busy. The special today was Cast Iron Beef Pot Pie. I had prepped a ton of them this morning, but we were whizzing through the supply. A few months ago, I had justified the purchase of forty personal-sized cast-iron skillets by rationalizing we could serve things like individual crème brulees and pot pie in them. But the truth was, I bought them because they were downright adorable. I loved that Magda brought them to the tables snugged in thick cloths, warning the customers that the pans were too hot to touch. Charming!

I stuck my head into the dining room again, trying to gauge from the flow of customers and the time of day how many more pot pies I should make. *Ten maybe?* I grabbed the bussing bin and took it back into the kitchen. I pulled ten tiny empty skillets out from among the dirty dishes, cleaned them quickly, then scooped a dollop of stew into each and topped them with pie shells. Into the oven! I had just set a timer when I heard Mrs. Seevers' voice. I walked out into the front.

"—heading to Costello's to pick up supplies for your next class. I have a list, but I didn't know what size of that New York strip steak to get." Bea smiled at Ava and me.

"That is a very good question, Mrs. Seevers," I said, "and the size of steak should depend on the quality of what is available at the market, and also how hungry you are. I'll teach you how to tell if a steak is done by feel, so size won't matter. But I'd say eight to ten ounces would be right on the money."

She wrote the information down on her list, nodding. I smiled at her, but then my face froze. Up on top of her head, where she had tucked them when she came in from the bright sunlight, was a pair of shiny new black sunglasses.

Bea Seevers? Sweet, thriving on gossip, lifelong resident of Leavensport Bea Seevers? What could she possibly have been doing in that field? I knew for a fact that she and her husband's retirement money was gone, thanks to an investment scheme cooked up by none other than Nestle. What if someone had promised her financial security? *Making good people do things they didn't want to do* ... was Bea one of those people?

"Okay, thanks! See you in class!" Mrs. Seevers trilled, turning to leave. My pot pie timer was going off. I made a mental note to add the sunglasses information to our I Spy Slides the first chance I got.

I hustled back to the kitchen, slipping on cat-shaped oven mitts, opening the oven, and pulling out ten flaky, golden-brown pot pies. *Perfection.* I put them on the cooling rack. They wouldn't be servable for another fifteen minutes, but it was okay. There were still two left from the first batch of the day.

Just then, Ava burst through the kitchen door with her phone in her hand. She somehow looked simultaneously enraged and overjoyed.

"Delilah texted!" Ava crowed. "She's back, she's at her house! I'm so relieved she's safe. I'm going to KILL her!"

I rolled my eyes. "Can I at least debrief her and add some notes to our I Spy Slides before you do?" I asked.

Ava made a face. "I suppose."

The lunch rush tapered off. About an hour before our shift ended, Carlos arrived, bursting with ideas for the dinner special. He began prepping ingredients enthusiastically.

I had exactly three pot pies left when the shift ended. I packed them in a cardboard box left over from one of our deliveries so that the three of us would have something to sustain us while we discussed Delilah's findings.

I leaned against the counter, watching Carlos chop and measure ingredients while I waited for Ava to finish cleaning tables, counting money, and rolling silverware. "What's for dinner, Carlos?" I asked.

"Oh, Jolie, too bad you are leaving." he said. "It is a Southwestern rice salad topped with the barbeque pork left over from a few nights ago. It is just ..." he put his hand on his chest and looked heavenward.

"Oh man," I said. "I am suddenly regretting all of the life choices that led to me already having dinner plans."

Carlos laughed heartily. "I will make it again for you sometime, Jolie."

"Whew! Good."

At that moment, I heard the bell on the front door ring and stuck my head into the front of the restaurant. Chief Tobias had pushed the door open and strode up to the counter.

"Hello, Teddy!" I exclaimed. "Are you here for dinner? Can I get you a menu?"

"Well, now," said Teddy. "It smells just amazing in here, but I actually came in to bring you back your laptop." He handed a plastic-wrapped package over the counter to me, and then extended a clipboard. "Will you sign here, confirming that you received your property?"

I laughed at Teddy's reluctant recitation of protocol and signed on the line.

"Thanks, Teddy."

"Okay, so, Tabitha put some tracking software on your laptop, and there is a search warrant in play, so everything on the laptop can be used by the Leavensport Police in this investigation."

I nodded. "Got it. Am I under obligation to inform the students of this?"

"No, not under a search warrant."

"Sounds good." I nodded again.

"And Tabitha will be in contact with you," he added. "She needs to be present at your next online class."

"Thanks for letting me know, Teddy. I appreciate all of your work on this."

Chief Tobias smiled and turned to go. Before he reached the door, Carlos, who had disappeared when the police chief had begun talking, reappeared with a to-go box, and handed it to him.

"Here's dinner for you, sir," Carlos said. "Thanks for keeping our village safe."

Teddy's jaw dropped, then he grinned. "Oh wow. Thank you. But as a police officer, I am not allowed to accept gifts." He eyed it and smiled regretfully.

"Can you accept it as a friend, then, not as a police officer?" asked Carlos.

"I think I can! Thanks, friend. I really can't wait to try it." He hustled out the door.

Carlos turned to me. "Of course, I will pay the price of the meal for the police chief. I just wanted him to have something for his dinner."

Tears sprang to my eyes at the heartfelt gesture. "No, Carlos, it's on the house. Like you said, he keeps our village safe. Don't worry, I won't say a word."

Ava appeared and we headed out. I followed her car over to her house, where we were supposed to meet Delilah, eat our carryout pot pies, and hear what Delilah had learned about the art commune. I drove along, studying the outline of Ava's puffy hair in the driver's seat of the car in front of me. A wave of nervousness hit me. Would this be a really emotional, private moment between the two of them? Should I back out gracefully? I could get the information from Delilah or Ava later.

Unfortunately, the drive was barely two minutes long if all of the lights in town were red, so we had arrived before I could formulate any sort of plan.

Delilah opened the door as we walked up. Ava leapt into her arms. I breathed a sigh of relief. Maybe this wouldn't be so bad.

Once inside, I busied myself setting the table and arranging the pot pies in their places. We all sat down and dug in.

"Mmmm ..." moaned Delilah. "I ate like a college student for less than twenty-four hours and I thought I was gonna die! I forgot what it was like. Ramen and toaster pastries. Sheesh!"

Ava chuckled. "Okay, so tell us everything."

"There is a LOT to tell," began Delilah.

I grabbed my laptop and opened a new slide. I was much faster at typing than writing.

"Okay, so I arrive, and it is a pretty typical college scene," Delilah started. I began typing. I wasn't sure what was important and what wasn't, so I tried to get as much as I could. "There are people hanging around, music playing, all that stuff. By the way, I have lots of pictures I snuck along the way—you can upload them later. I drove up and parked, then I walked up to a group of them. There were three girls, Linzie, Allison, and Lahiri."

"Lahiri!" I interrupted. "She's in our class." Ava shushed me and Delilah continued.

"So, I start talking to them and they say there is going to be a bonfire in the backyard once the sun goes down and I can stay and hang out. I started telling them my back story. They are really nice and sympathetic and we get along really well."

"Her back story," Ava explained, "is that she was a business major but she loves to paint, so she switched majors and her parents are really mad at her and are refusing to pay for anything so she has nowhere to stay." I nodded.

"So, the commune is three big old Victorian houses in this little mini-neighborhood out in the middle of nowhere. Like, it is surrounded by woods. Linzie, Lahiri, and Allison live in one of the three houses. It is called Painters' House, and that is usually where the students who are majoring in painting live. Linzie and Allison are painters, but Lahiri is a cultural arts major.

All three of the houses have little nicknames. Like I said, ours is Painters' House, and the middle one, the one where Darla died, is called The Office. That's because Quinn lives there. Quinn Kingsley. He is the one who founded the Sanctuary for Creative Minds. His parents are really rich. His mother is a big producer in Hollywood.

They bought him the property for cheap, and he fixed it up and started this commune for art students. Allison really admires him. She went on and on about how he believes that artists are the prophets for society and we should set ourselves apart and realize we are superior to everyone else, and that we have a duty to bring truth and beauty to humanity."

"That sounds a little cult-ish to me," commented Ava.

Delilah nodded. "Yeah, it kinda felt that way. The Quinn guy is talked about like he is some sort of god. But anyway, that is why the middle house is called The Office, because that's where Quinn lives. Quinn, a girl named Poppy, and Darla, the girl that was murdered, lived in The Office."

I was typing non-stop.

"Last, the third house is called 'The Magic Cave.' It is the oldest house and the most run-down. The living room is huge, so that is where they hold all of the parties. I think that's where they came up with the name. Three people live there, too, A girl named Alyssa, a girl named Mod, and a boy named Tad. I think Alyssa and Tad are dating, but I'm not sure."

I was pretty sure my fingers were going to fall off, I was typing so fast.

"So, we stayed at this bonfire for a while. I talked to the others a little bit. They all seemed sad about the murder. I never saw Quinn. We had a few drinks and watched the fire die down. Linzie and Allison told me about how Linzie is graduating at the end of the semester, so there will be a room open. I told her I was interested in applying for it. We talked a little more, I told them my backstory, and they acted like I was a good candidate to fill the spot.

"It was getting late, so I added the bit about not having a place to stay. The three girls had kind of a discreet huddle, then came and offered to let me stay on the couch, which of course I took them up on. I was all set up with blankets. Linzie got me a glass of wine and we were all talking. Then, once

Lahiri and Allison went to bed, Linzie suggested we sneak over to look at Darla's bedroom. She told me she was the one who found Darla's body. She had just finished posting on her vlog and came over to the kitchen in the other house to look for something in the fridge, she said. Hold on." Delilah paused and dug a piece of paper out of her pocket. "I wrote down the web address for her vlog so we can look at it." She handed it to Ava.

"Hey, smart move!" I said.

"Anyway, as we were walking over to the other house to get to Darla's room," continued Delilah, "Linzie told me that one time, she went over to Darla's room to bring her back a sweatshirt she had borrowed and found Darla and Tad together. They weren't doing anything, but it was still strange. I thought that might be important."

"Yeah! That is a huge detail!" I exclaimed, typing it on the slide. "If they were having an affair, that puts Tad in a suspicious light."

"What was Darla's room like?" asked Ava.

"It is all marked off with police tape, but we went in and poked around. Her family must be rich because she had a lot of nice stuff. Designer clothes, a big flat-screen television on the wall, expensive bedding. I wasn't expecting it. Everyone else seemed kind of ... bohemian, I guess? But her room was like walking into ... I don't know ... a princess's room. Linzie told me the car outside, the two-seater convertible, that was hers, too. I think she must have come from a wealthy family. She had lots of polaroid pictures of herself. They all are very retro in a lot of ways. She always had torn jeans on with black hose underneath. I don't know if that is a rich kid thing or just a personal statement?"

"That was really useful information," I said. "Thank you for putting yourself in harm's way to help out this investigation."

"Oh, I'm so glad I could help," replied Delilah. "The idea of someone so young dying ... and in such a horrid way!" She shuddered. "I'll spend as much time in that art commune as I need to get the information that you need."

Ava leaned forward. "Did you get any sort of gut feeling while you were there? Any sense of something going on?"

Delilah nodded. "Actually, yes. They pretend like everyone is equal, like it is a commune with equal shares, but Quinn definitely calls the shots. And the weird thing is, some of them still seem to worship the ground he walks on. Allison is one of them. You should have seen the look she got on her face talking about him."

"Well, what is your plan from here on out?" I asked Delilah.

"I can go back tomorrow, see how far into that organization I can get, see what information I can find," she declared. "I have this strange feeling that what I have seen so far is just the tip of the iceberg."

"Important question," I said, "do you think it's safe?"

"I think if I keep my wits about me, I will be just fine." Delilah assured us.

It seemed like we had all of the useful information. That just about wrapped it up for the night. I saved the document and started to power down my laptop.

Then, out of nowhere, Ava grabbed both of Delilah's hands. "Hey, last night scared me. I didn't know if you were dead, I didn't know anything."

Ava's voice turned angry. "The last thing you said to me was 'don't text back you'll blow my cover'??"

I grabbed my bag and walked quietly to the door, allowing them to finish their discussion in private. As I slipped out, I heard Delilah whispering, "I know, I'm sorry. I promise."

I walked through Ava's backyard and through my own door, and was greeted by a mob of cats. I sat on the floor right there in the kitchen, squeezing and cuddling them. There is nothing more soothing than the love of kitties. I scooped out a late dinner for all of them, which they scarfed almost before I had turned around.

"Babies want whipped cream?" I asked. My cats had a thing for Redi Whip. I had to always keep some on hand. They'd come running when they heard the *tschhhh* of the can and I put a small dollop on the floor for them to lap up.

"Reeeoooooowwwwww," came an affirmative chorus. "Reeeoooooowwwwww!"

I went to the refrigerator and pulled out the can. I squirted four generous blobs a few feet apart, one for each cat. They homed in on their blob and began contentedly licking at it. Bobbi Jo had cream in her whiskers almost immediately. Oh, well. Those cuties deserved something special. I had been so busy lately I wasn't giving them the love they deserved. They seemed to have forgiven me, though. I wonder if that trick worked for people. I should keep a can of whipped cream in my bag just in case.

Chapter Nine

As worries about murder filled my mind, a mouthwatering aroma filled my kitchen. It was our second (uninterrupted) online class, and we were cooking steak. Ava had given pointers on what to look for when purchasing steak at the butcher, how to season, and the differences in the cooking temperatures, from rare to well-done. Then I had stepped in and given my usual safety tips about preheating the pan and began to demonstrate cooking a New York strip steak to perfection.

It hadn't been very long since the unplanned meeting to decide if we should continue the class after Darla's murder, so I wondered if some students would skip class, but a few minutes before class started, they had begun popping onto my monitor one at a time. Bea's screen had stayed blank, and she had typed, "Girls, my camera isn't working but I can see and hear you just fine," into the chat. I had remembered what the back of the receipt for the sunglasses had said: *Skip class or camera off so no one can see*. What was she hiding?

"That's fine, let us know if you have questions,"

I had written back and had given the camera a thumbs up.

All of the students had shown up, and were quiet but attentive. They didn't know that the police had a search warrant and had installed spyware on the laptop that would record the class session. Tabitha, working for the police, sat just out of sight of the cameras, watching the laptop. Technically, she was there to monitor the equipment and make any adjustments needed; however, she was also a full-time therapist, so I guessed that all of the students' vocal inflections and facial expressions were being noted by her watchful eye.

"It is important to let the steak rest before serving." I gestured to the foil tent that I had instructed them to place over the steak once they had transferred it to the plate. "Cooking drives the moisture into the center of the meat. If you allow five to ten minutes for the steak to rest, the moisture redistributes and rehydrates the protein fibers—and bingo!" I pulled the tent off with a flourish. "Perfect steak!" Bradley zoomed the camera in on the plate.

We wrapped up the session and signed off. We were all pretty happy that it had gone off without a hitch. Tabitha collected her equipment and departed without much discussion. I wondered if it was difficult for her to separate Therapist Tabitha from Investigator Tabitha.

Next class we were teaching the side dishes: glazed carrots and parmesan asparagus. But getting through this session was one big thing off of my list for the week. Tomorrow was the town hall meeting. Carlos and the front staff agreed to cover us so Ava and I could attend.

The next day, I bustled around my house, determined not to be late for the meeting. I twisted my hair up and pinned it in place with a large hair clip. Lip gloss, mascara. I slipped into black leggings and ankle boots, then walked back into my bedroom where the burgundy blouse I had laid across my bed had a cat lounging on top of it.

"Why, Juju Bean, why?" I groaned, shooing my kitty away and picking long black hairs off of my top before putting it on. I was pretty sure they had kitty meetings to decide which cat should sit on which item to make sure the cat hairs showed up the most.

I gave myself one last look in the mirror. I wondered briefly if Meiser would be at the meeting and watched my cheeks turn pink at the thought. *Eesh.* I was packing my bag when I heard the front door bang open.

"I thought you didn't want to be late!" called Ava, "Let's go!"

"I'm ready!" This town meeting wasn't a potluck, as some of them were, so we didn't have to bring a lot of food with us, and we had decided to walk over. It would be nice to get fresh air.

"I'm ready, let's go!"

We hustled to Leavensport Community Center which was in the heart of town, close to Cast Iron Creations. It was a lovely space. Mayor Nalini had seen to it being refurbished a few years ago, and the warm sunny interior was elegant with wooden benches and faux marble floors. We came in as people were getting settled. There was quite a crowd. I knew the main concern around town was the land that was up for sale and how it would change our village. There were always one or two other items. Our little town was rowdy, though, and people tended to speak their minds at these meetings. Hopefully this one wouldn't go off the rails.

"Where should we sit?" asked Ava. She spotted Delilah and waved at her. She headed our way, weaving around townspeople while fiddling on her phone. Just as she put her phone back in her pocket, mine vibrated in my bag. *Had she messaged me?* I needed to find a way to slip away and check my phone without Ava looking over my shoulder. My stomach twisted at this new need for deception.

"The Tuckers are in the center section, over there." Delilah gestured to wooden benches that were directly in front of the raised stage with the podium where Mayor Nalini always stood. About midway back, I could see Grandma Opal's latest hairdo through the crowd. We made our way over and sat down with them.

"There you girls are!" said Aunt Fern. "This is gonna be a good meeting. The mayor is doing a good job." She glanced up at the podium adoringly. I wondered how their date had gone. Not horribly, it seemed. I noticed Grandma's face looked sour. Mayor Nalini was calling everyone to order.

"What's wrong with Grandma?" I asked Aunt Fern. She pointed. A few rows in front of us sat Uncle Eddie and his whole family—his wife and all of their children, including Tink. I guessed Grandma and my family still weren't totally getting along.

We settled and got quiet and the mayor began to speak. He said that they would be discussing a variety of topics, all centering around Leavensport's economic growth in the future.

"I have asked one of our village's pillars, longtime resident Bea Seevers, to collect some information on the local businesses at the 'street' level, if you will. She is going to present her findings to us now, to cast some light on the local economy. I will now give the podium to Mrs. Bea Seevers, thank you."

The polite clapping that began to welcome her sputtered out as she walked across the stage. She was dressed smartly, in a crisp baby-blue pant suit and a blouse, but she was wearing her new black sunglasses indoors.

Mayor Nalini looked at her oddly before taking a chair to watch her present. There were little murmurs in the crowd but no one said anything. Mrs. Seevers seemed determined to act like nothing was amiss.

"Why is she wearing sunglasses?" Ava hissed to me.

"How should I know? But it is weird!" I hissed back.

"Ladies and gentlemen," began Bea, "a few weeks ago, I handed out a survey to all of the small businesses in Leavensport. Thank you for completing those and getting them back to me."

"Hey, are you okay?" shouted out a woman from the crowd.

Bea's mouth pursed up as if she had eaten a lemon. "I am perfectly fine, ma'am, and I'm not sure what you're talking about," she snapped.

"Wait, did she give us a survey?" I whispered to Ava.

"Yeah, like two weeks ago!"

"You didn't mention it to me!"

"Didn't think you cared, that's front of the house stuff."

I shrugged. She was right.

Mrs. Seevers continued her presentation, discussing the local economy. From what she was saying, it sounded like things were going okay, but there was not a ton of growth. We were doing just fine, in my opinion. Bea wrapped up and everyone clapped politely as she left the stage, her sunglasses still on her face. I was itching to add her strange behavior to our I Spy Slides.

Mayor Nalini took the podium. Before he could even begin to speak, a voice came from the back of the audience. "What can you tell us about the sale on the land?" It sounded like Margy, the receptionist at the courthouse. There were murmurs in the crowd, agreeing with her.

Mayor Nalini put up his hand to quiet them, but Uncle Eddie interrupted again. "And what about the holes out in that field by the M&M restaurant? Did the police go out there and look at them? Why are they there? Did that have something to do with the sale?"

"Oh, just be quiet, Eddie!" Grandma Opal burst out. "I don't even know why you're asking! You don't live in our town!"

"Grandma, shhhh!" I hissed. Grandma Opal fell silent but sat up straight in her chair, eyes forward, a displeased expression on her face.

"Listen, folks, the sale of the land isn't set in stone yet," said the mayor. "There are a lot of moving parts, and I am not at liberty to share everything with you all yet. But everything is going to be fine. Everything we're working on is to help make Leavensport a better place."

"So, what's happening? Are we just going to end up a suburb of Tri-City?" interrupted another voice.

"Crime is on the rise!" someone shouted. The crowd seemed restless.

"Listen, things change," hedged the mayor. "That is unavoidable. But we will always be Leavensport. You heard Mrs. Seevers, our economy is decent, but there is so much room for growth! I can't tell you anything specific at this time, but I will."

"And those holes?" demanded one of the Zimmerman brothers.

"Ted—the police—have checked the situation with the holes out, and they are just holes," he insisted. "Let's stay calm. Someone got bored and had a shovel. Kids maybe. We have increased police patrols in the area to keep an eye on it."

I turned around and scanned the crowd. Not too far away, Teddy sat next to Tabitha. They were huddled together, talking. He glanced up when the mayor made this comment and nodded awkwardly.

The mayor continued delivering his speech in bursts, pausing to field shouted questions. I started to zone out. We weren't going to learn anything about what was going on with those holes here.

"Hey, let me out," I whispered to Ava, "I need to go to the bathroom." I squeezed past her and Delilah and went down the aisle toward the back. On the way out, I noticed Keith and Lydia sitting together. *Interesting!* Once I got into the restroom, I checked my phone. Sure enough, the message was from Delilah.

Ava works tomorrow and you don't. Can we meet to go over our Nestle investigation? It needs to be tomorrow because I was planning on going back to the art commune tomorrow night and staying there for a few days.

Yes, that sounds good, I messaged back. *Let's meet at the gallery at nine.* My gut squirmed a little at hiding things from my best friend.

I came out of the restroom and went back into the auditorium. I walked around in the back, scoping out who was there. A few late-comers stood around, not wanting to annoy people by finding a seat. I didn't see Meiser, which was disappointing.

I looked to my right. Nestle! He was standing with a tall, broad-shouldered man. Was that Meiser? No, it just looked a lot like him. I took a deep breath and walked over to the pair. Nestle looked up and saw me, getting his usual look of disgust on his face. This man was not in my fan club to say the least. Although I wasn't in his, either.

"Hi, there, Mr. Nestle." I tried to keep the dislike out of my voice. "Taking an interest in the local economy, are we?"

"Miss Tucker," Nestle replied through gritted teeth. "Yes, it is good to stay informed, don't you think? You can't seem to stand it when you don't know everything about everything."

"Got that right!" I retorted.

"Miss Tucker, this is Miles Milano, former mayor of Tri-City. Miles, this is Jolie Tucker, local pain in the butt."

I reached out and firmly shook the man's hand, while glaring at Nestle due to that little snide comment. *So, this was the other brother. The one who had sent Meiser to Leavensport in the first place, to see if there was any land that could be bought up for development.* He definitely resembled his brother in the looks department.

"Are you involved in the land transaction they are talking about?" I tried to sound calm and professional to see what information I could get out of him. It was certainly telling that he was here, at this meeting, with Nestle by his side.

Miles shrugged. "I am just here as an observer, seeing where the chips fall. It is nice to meet the lady that my brother has taken a fancy to." He flashed a plastic smile at me, then turned to Nestle. "Jackson, I'll call you later." Then he strode out of the nearest exit.

The meeting ended and people drifted away. I headed home, quickly adding that I had seen Nestle with Miles at the meeting about the land sale to my secret notebook about Nestle, and then spent the rest of the evening on the couch, watching TV with the cats.

The next morning, I met Delilah in the office of her art gallery. I had almost stopped by the restaurant to fry up some of our donuts to bring with me, but I didn't think I had it in me to look Ava in the eye and give her some fictitious story of what I was going to do that day. Instead, I stopped by Costello's for some bagels and cream cheese and a pint of ripe strawberries.

Delilah and I sat nibbling for a moment while my laptop started up. Everything was quiet, since the gallery was closed during the day and open on evenings and weekends. Delilah was always over at Crafty's Corner, selling art supplies or teaching art workshops during the day.

"Is it okay for you to take time off from the shop?" I asked as I chewed.

"Yeah, I've got a few hours. I have someone covering the counter and there aren't any workshops today."

"Okay. So, let's dig in," I began. "I'll be honest. I have a ton of suspicions, a ton of gut instincts, and a ton of circumstantial evidence, but nothing concrete as of now."

"I just want to know what he is up to." Delilah sighed. "My parents gave me all of this," she gestured around herself to indicate the gallery and shop two doors down, "and I'm afraid if I can't outwit him, he'll take it all away. Plus, Ava would never forgive me for giving him the upper hand by selling to him! We would be over. I don't want to lose her."

"First of all, who knows what would have happened if you hadn't gotten the money for the blackmailers in the DR? You did what you had to do." I opened the notebook. "The pattern that I see is that Nestle is everywhere. He is involved in everything. He knows too much of everyone's business. He has too much influence. Did you see him at the town meeting? He was there with Miles Milano, the old mayor of Tri-City. The one who was looking into buying up Leavensport land for development? Remember?"

"I do remember. You think him wanting my place is part of something bigger?" Delilah's voice wavered. "Maybe we should see what we can learn about him, maybe both of them."

I was already opening a search engine in a browser window on my laptop. "Exactly what I was thinking! Okay. Nestle. Yesterday, Miles called him Jackson. Do you know if that is his first name?" I asked.

"Hold on, his full name is on the paperwork for the sale of a share of the gallery." Delilah jumped up and pulled open the filing cabinet. Unlike the art shop, Crafty's Corner, the gallery and its office were sparkling clean and neat as a pin. It was like there were two versions of Delilah. Within a few seconds, she pulled out a paper and read from it. "Jackson Nestle. That's him."

"Jackson Nestle. Okay. Let's see what comes up." I began to sift through the hits of pictures of people of the same name, as well as shady websites that offered his address and history for a fee. I scanned through the images. A few that were definitely not him. A few old men, one woman, even an extremely adorable cocker spaniel in Switzerland claimed the name. "That's him!" I clicked on a picture of a slightly younger looking him. "This is just an article about him being involved in politics in Tri-City. I'm going to keep looking."

Delilah leaned over my shoulder as I clicked around. "Ooh, check this out!" I crowed. "He has a criminal record in Canada! Canada? Seriously?" According to public record, Nestle was a business owner who was found guilty of tax evasion. He did time in a white-collar prison.

"Holy smokes!" shouted Delilah. "He's a criminal! I knew it!"

Now we're getting somewhere! I typed his name, "Canada", " tax evasion", and "prison" into the search bar and an article came up from a news source. "Here's an article saying that his third ex-wife testified against him in court. It was a huge deal. That was what brought him down. She went into witness protection right after the trial." I looked up, thinking. "Man. There would be no way of finding her, but that is a woman I would love to ask a few questions." I shook my head, writing her name down in my notebook.

"Yeah! Number one, what were you thinking, marrying that jerk?" snorted Delilah.

I laughed out loud. "Let's search Miles Milano and see what we can find," I pressed on. "They were as thick as thieves at the town meeting."

"Ha! Possibly literally!" hooted Delilah.

"Okay, I'm getting a lot of articles from when he was mayor, just normal mayor stuff ..." I went back and added in a few more keywords. "Huh. He doesn't have a criminal record anywhere that I can find," I announced.

But the name Milano came up a ton. There were Milanos in Italy, in New York, and here in Ohio. And many of them had been involved in illegal activity that was associated with organized crime. Miles had managed to keep his hands clean, but that could just mean that he hadn't been caught. Yet.

"So, in conclusion, Nestle has a criminal record and hangs out with men from international crime families. I think we can safely say he is up to something." I looked sideways at Delilah. It was good that we were finding things out, that got us closer, but learning that the man she was up against was a real criminal was unsettling.

Delilah glanced at the clock. "Okay, we should wrap this up. I have some things I need to get done before Ava gets off of work so she and I can hang out for an hour or so before I go back undercover at the art commune."

I nodded and began packing up my things. This was going to be one interesting notebook entry!

Chapter Ten

Ava had seemed much more relaxed when we sent Delilah off for this round of undercover work a few days ago. This time, we had a plan. The rest of the week passed smoothly. The restaurant was busy, and when I was home, I read the book Tabitha had recommended, *Girl, Wash Your Face.*

I needed to get back to therapy soon. This book had some great parts to it and I planned to journal about some thoughts I had that I wanted to talk to Tabitha about concerning this book—the chapter about women being defined by their weight gave me some laugh-out-loud moments. I had some takeaways for sure that I wanted to share. Her message was positive and empowering, although I didn't see eye-to-eye with her completely. For example, not everyone had the opportunities a white woman raised in a certain faith has, and that never came up in the book. It's also nothing I know about coming from privilege, but I've grown up with an amazing Latino woman who I've had to watch go through some serious racist experiences in education, social situations, and I've watched people stereotype her for being Latino as well as her choice in relationships—and, I do not like that. I made a few mental notes and then grabbed my journal bullet pointing those thoughts for a journal entry later.

Speaking of my bestie, today was one of the few days Ava and I were both off from the restaurant, but we would be running our tails off anyway. Delilah was due back from her undercover work any second now, and this evening was our third cooking class. My phone buzzed. Ava. *Delilah's back, want to debrief at the gallery?* I scooped up the last of my scrambled eggs and took the last sip of my coconut chai tea before I stuffed my laptop into my bag and hurried out to the car.

Delilah always looked artsy but today there was no mistaking. She wore paint-spattered overalls and half a dozen mismatched bead necklaces. She had a lovely multicolored scarf wrapped around her waist, and a slouchy hat on her long brown hair. She even had a paintbrush behind one ear.

Since there were three of us, Delilah pulled a fold-up card table out of a closet and arranged chairs around it. Ava opened a carryout box of fried donuts that were still warm from Cast Iron Creations and set it on the table in the middle of all of us. Everyone grabbed one, even me, who had already had breakfast. Those things are spectacular!

I popped open my laptop and clicked on the I Spy Slides file.

"So, Delilah, tell us of your adventures at the Sanctuary for Creative Minds," Ava intoned with a dramatic flourish of her arm.

"Well, Allison, Linzie, and Lahiri were really friendly again. Allison cleaned out a drawer for me to keep things in. They said they are going to approach the group about letting me apply for the spot when Linzie graduates at the end of the semester."

"Is there a formal process for new housemates?" I asked.

"Not really, I think they have to vote on it," explained Delilah. "But I am getting the vibe that if Quinn says no, you're out, and if Quinn says yes, you're in. And, of course, it's a commune, so you have to agree to go in on everything. They split utilities and the grocery bill and take turns cleaning the houses. Everything is supposedly even and fair."

"I want to know more about this Quinn guy," I said. "He definitely rules the roost."

"I found out he is a Teacher's Assistant, working on a graduate degree in art, focus on blacksmithing," added Delilah. "It isn't an official major at the art college in Triopolis University, but his parents put pressure on the school so they found a blacksmith to apprentice him. He studies with that guy while he takes his other classes and he'll graduate with a master's in art."

"Sounds to me like Quinn is used to getting what he wants," I commented. I added this information to his slide.

Ava leaned forward and grabbed another donut. "Did you find out anything else?" she asked with her mouth full. At that moment, a buzzer sounded, startling all of us.

"That's the doorbell for the delivery entrance. I've got to sign for this, I'll be right back." Delilah hopped up and dashed away. I stared after her, lost in thought. Deliveries and shipments. There must be a lot of moving parts in a gallery. Delilah reappeared.

"Okay, where was I?" She thought for a moment. "That's right. Something very interesting. They had another fire in the fire pit and everyone was hanging out. Allison had had a few glasses of wine and then told me that Darla told her that she and Tad are sleeping together, even though Tad is dating Alyssa. I already knew that, because Linzie told me. But what she said next was interesting. Allison said that Darla wanted him to break up with Alyssa, and when he wouldn't, she threatened to tell her about the affair."

"Oh my gosh!" shrieked Ava. "Pretty sure that is a solid-gold motive for murder." Then she looked skeptical. "Are you sure she wasn't making it up?"

Delilah shook her head. "After she told me that she freaked out and begged me not to tell anyone. She said Alyssa still doesn't know. She said she didn't mention it when the police came and got statements from everyone."

"Why the heck didn't she?" I wondered.

"She said she got scared and clammed up. I believe her. Trust me, she was telling no lies at that point. Right after that, she started drunk crying and we had to put her to bed." Delilah rolled her eyes.

I clicked on Tad's slide in our I Spy Slides and typed in this new information. This certainly put him at the top of the suspect list.

"Well done, once again, Delilah!" I congratulated her. "Great spy work!"

Ava nodded, leaning her head on Delilah's shoulder.

"We also need to add a slide on Bea Seevers," I said, clicking around on my screen. "She has been acting downright bizarre lately."

"Yeah, wearing those sunglasses during the meeting?" Ava said.

"And I found the receipt for them out in the field by Mick's restaurant, where those weird holes were dug. It had her writing on the back of it!"

"You did? I didn't know that," said Ava. "Wait, what were you doing in the field?"

I blanched, realizing that it connected to my side investigation of Nestle. "Er, just checking it out, you know? It's a mystery. Weird holes ... in a field." I was a terrible liar.

"Yeah," mused Ava. "People seem to think Nestle is connected to those holes in some way. What do you think of all of that, Delilah?"

Delilah suddenly choked on a bite of donut and began to cough. Ava jumped up and thumped her on the back.

"You okay, honey?" she asked Delilah, who nodded, red-faced.

"Anyway," I said, hoping to steamroll past that awkwardness, "Bea had written on the back of the receipt 'Skip class or camera off so one can see.' Now what the heck does that mean?"

"Oh wow, that is odd," agreed Delilah.

"I wonder if she is tangled up in this somehow through the cooking class," Ava said.

"I sure hope not, but that is pretty weird." I closed my laptop. "We'll have to see if she turns her camera on for the next class. Anyway, that's all I have. I had better get going. Stay safe and keep your eyes open, ladies. And thanks again, Delilah, for going undercover for us."

Delilah smiled and nodded.

I packed up and headed out. We had our

cooking class in a few hours and I wanted to check my ingredients list one last time. As soon as I was outside the door, though, I stopped and texted Delilah. *Email me a list of what Nestle is involved in with the gallery.*

I was very curious about what aspects of the gallery Nestle had his slimy tentacles around.

"Oh my goodness, look at all you beautiful cooks! You look amazing! We are thrilled to have you here!" trilled Ava, beginning our third online class. From watching her, you would never know we were in the middle of a murder investigation, with an investigator sitting in the room with us, watching every move, while we taught a class on a laptop that was chock full of spyware ...

Suddenly my heart froze. I was such an idiot. The laptop. It was recording everything done on it. I thought about my browsing history over the last few days. Searches on Nestle, Miles, the Milano family, the mafia, criminal records ... who would see that search history? Tabitha? Teddy? Would Meiser see it? My heart started up again, but was thundering in my chest. What was I going to do?

"Jolie? JOLIE?" Ava was staring at me.

"Sorry, what?" I came back to reality, realizing it was my turn to talk.

"I think you were about to introduce the dishes for today," she urged.

"Oh, yes, of course!" I said, plastering on a smile. I quickly reviewed the main points of cooking steak from the class before, then began the steps for making the side dishes. Today's class covered glazed carrots and parmesan asparagus—elegant side dishes that pair perfectly with steak.

I slid the cast-iron skillet with the asparagus into the oven and stepped aside for Ava to demonstrate preparing the glazed carrots. I scooted off camera to get a drink from my water bottle and glance at the monitor.

All of the students were working hard on their side dishes. Bea's camera was on, and her sunglasses were gone. She looked fine. Mod, on the other hand, seemed to be suffering from a cold or allergies. Her eyes were red and her face was blotchy. She paused cooking for a moment to cough. Everything was in bloom, that made sense. *Poor gal, she should take some allergy medicine.*

Ava pulled the parmesan asparagus out of the oven and began plating the two sides. It was about seven minutes before the end of the session. Time to wrap things up to allow five minutes at the end for any questions.

Bradley zoomed in on the plate to show the glazed carrots and asparagus in all their glory.

"Now, with all meals, timing is everything. You'll have to plan exactly when to put the steak on the heat so that it will be resting right when the side dishes are do—"

Ava's speech was interrupted when the screen on the laptop went black and we saw the blue squiggly line again.

"No, not again!" I heard one of the students scream.

Tabitha leapt to her feet, then began clicking the mouse and hitting keys, trying to trace it, all to no avail. "The session has been hacked again. I can't seem to get through this firewall," she shouted.

Once again, the figure appeared against a black

background, wearing the upside-down face mask and black-and-white striped shirt. Picasso's Peril!

"I enjoyed watching your class today," the distorted voice uttered, "and the food looks delicious. Too bad one of you won't be around next week to enjoy dessert!"

Chapter Eleven

Ava and I met Peggy and Gemma at Gemma's Bohemian Jewelry store the following day to see if Gemma, tech wizard she was, could provide us with more information than Tabitha was willing to share.

We walked into the store and I wanted to buy everything. Gemma stood with a long flowing caftan dress that had bold red and yellow prints with a matching tignon that allowed her long dreads to be highlighted. Decked out in her own jewelry, she was stunning—one of the most beautiful women I'd ever seen.

"Whoa, you both look super serious and super stressed to the max," Peggy's gaze flitted across both our faces in concern.

"So much has happened. We need your help."

"Maybe we should grab some pie and get caught up," Gemma said.

We sat down and I immediately dug into my blueberry pie without missing a beat. Ava started filling the ladies in on what Delilah had found out,

Tabitha adding some sort of techie spyware to my computer, the murder, and everything else that had taken place.

"Yikes," Gemma said.

"Exactly," I said with a mouthful of pie.

"Show some manners," Ava squawked at me.

Peggy giggled. "Well, I'd say you came to the right place. I'm sure Gemma can work her magic and figure something out. She can do just about anything when it comes to computers."

"You make me sound like a cybercriminal," Gemma blurted out with a mouthful of apple pie.

We all saw the irony of what just happened and cracked up.

"Will Tabitha or anyone that is monitoring this know what you are doing?" I asked concerned mostly from my mistake of forgetting before I searched things that could get me in trouble with Meiser.

"Not if I do it correctly," Gemma winked at me.

I handed my laptop off into Gemma's capable hands.

Peggy was kind enough to get us seconds and I opted for the chocolate cream this time. I looked across the street and began backhanding Ava's shoulder.

"Child, what IS your problem?"

"Look who it is," I said pointing.

Ava squinted her eyes, "Why is he everywhere?"

Nestle and Mayor Cardinal were looking at an old apartment building and Nestle carried a clipboard and was taking notes on whatever the good mayor of Tri-City was saying.

"I don't know, but every time I see that guy, my stomach sinks."

Peggy brought more pie to the table. I was starting to get full, but I knew I could always handle more sweets.

"Isn't that the mayor over there?" I pointed.

"Yep, he and his crew have been hanging around these parts a lot lately. Gemma and I have decided to start attending the Tri-City assembly meetings to find out what is going on. He's even graced us with his presence trying the pie, talking about what 'cute' shops we girls run." Peggy air quoted "cute" for emphasis.

"I love it when men call women entrepreneurs 'girls,'" I hissed, rolling my eyes.

"Right? Whoever that guy is with him was nosing around last week back in the purse section of the shop."

"Nestle was shopping for a purse?" Ava's eyes bulged to full capacity.

"Not a purse, he was asking about a baby bag. Someone in his family is due soon."

"Wow, you make it sound like he has a heart or something," I said.

"I've seen him with the mayor a lot, so I thought he was making it all up to gather some intel for whatever they are up to."

"You make a good point. I wouldn't put it past him," Ava said.

I nodded.

"The city has changed a lot in the last few years. Prior to this mayor, the previous guy, Milano, resigned. He said he left office due to family issues, but there was a lot of buzz that he was up to no good. Reporters were starting to sniff around, and a local guy that runs a popular blog wrote something that suggested he was looking to gentrify the city and work to get rid of those in poverty and the homeless."

"Really!" My voice rose three octaves in fascination.

"Milano, that's—" Ava started.

"Mick's brother," I finished for her.

"Oooo, who is this Mick? He sounds hot," Peggy leaned forward, making her ponytail sway around her shoulders.

I laughed, "Now, how does saying a name make a guy hot?"

"I saw it in your eyes," Peggy chortled.

"Oh man, you have this one pegged!" Ava laughed, pushing on my arm.

I chose to ignore them with a slight grin. "What's interesting is that we have the term 'urban sprawl' being thrown around our town with a lot of land up for sale that connects to the highway into Tri-City. Nestle is lurking around our town, too. Now, he's here with politicians where the word 'gentrification' is being thrown around?"

Ava and I looked at each other knowingly. We knew this was going to go on the I Spy Slides somewhere. I had to talk to Delilah. I couldn't keep up this lie with Ava. It was making me sick.

"So, do you know anything more about the group of college kids?" Ava asked Peggy.

"They have been coming in here about once a week to work on projects for school. It's always on a Friday afternoon. I'm happy to make sure I'm always here and do a bit of probing for you, if you'd like. I know you said you have Ava's inside gal on the case." Peggy and Ava exchanged a smile.

"That would be wonderful if you are able to gather any new information. I kind of have a bet going with someone on who can figure this all out first."

"Would it happen to be with that hottie, Mick?" Peggy guessed.

"Jolie and Mick sitting in a tree," Ava sang.

Luckily, Gemma popped back and said, "We are good to go on my end. I'm all set up. I'll need a bit of time to look through things then I'll get back with you."

Later that week, on Saturday morning, Delilah met Ava, Peggy, and Gemma and me at Cast Iron Creations. I was excited to have Peggy and Gemma come visit our village and check out our restaurant.

"This place is so adorable!" Gemma exclaimed looking around. "I absolutely love that wall mural."

"My girlfriend did that," Ava smiled broadly at Delilah.

"You are extremely talented," Peggy said, looking over the wall-sized painting of the village.

"Wow, thanks. You all are making me blush!" Delilah put both hands across her cheeks trying to hide the flush.

I noticed the restaurant was more packed than normal. There was a table with a woman seated by herself that seemed extremely close to our four-top. I didn't recognize this elderly lady from the village, but I assumed she was an out-of-towner.

"So, who has updates?" I asked giving Delilah an out from her embarrassment.

"I'll start." Delilah pulled a notebook from her artsy canvas tote.

"Wow, someone's even taking notes!" Ava laughed, catching my eye and jerking her head in Delilah's direction.

"I've learned from my PI girlfriend."

"Okay, enough with all the cute stuff. We get it. You two are *adorable*. Now let's get to the good stuff." I grinned at them. Peggy and Gemma followed suit.

"Righto my cap-ee-tain!" Delilah joked, flipping to her most recent notes. "Some of the things that stood out to me this last week are that one, Tad and Alyssa are *not* happy together. That man has serious anger issues."

"Shocking," Ava said.

Magda had interrupted us briefly to take our order. The place was hopping this morning and I had grabbed drinks and fried donuts to tide us over and told Magda to take her time and get to us when she could.

"Sorry, it's been nonstop in here this morning," she said, wiping her brow.

"Why? What's so special about today?" Ava looked around.

"Yesterday was the last day of school. Most of our customers this morning are Leavensport school staff celebrating."

We all looked at each other and laughed. "Right, educators would celebrate the following morning after going home and falling straight into bed!" I said.

"I know I would—dealing with kids all day long every single day for nine months straight! I don't know how any of our teachers put up with us!"

"Great teachers are the foundation of society!" Gemma exclaimed. "My grandma and my mom were both educators. The ones that care and work hard. I thought about it. I don't have that need to be underpaid and underappreciated though. I don't know how they do it."

"Um, I'm going to interrupt to ask about the breakfast special. The deep-fried cast iron cinnamon donuts are amazing. I'm going to try to find a way to turn this into a pie," Peggy said looking at me.

"I'll give you the recipe."

"Today's special is . . ." Magda paused, her lips turned to a small grin as she looked at me, "Carlos' Cast Iron Breakfast Skillet. It's got—"

"Whoa, whoa, whoa, Carlos'—where is that man?" I said jokingly.

"You're the one who told him to take more control!" Magda's eyes lit up with humor.

"I'm kidding. What did the genius cast iron chef come up with today?"

"This has everything but the kitchen sink in it—and I wouldn't be surprised if customers aren't eating it and texting their friends about it and that's why we are so busy. Let's see. It's got Spanish chorizo, eggs, red potatoes, garlic, chillies, onions, and—"

"Sold!" Gemma and Peggy said in unison slamming their menus down.

"Yeah, I take it all back —Carlos is a true genius. I'm having that," I said as Ava and Delilah's eyes bulged out and they nodded in agreement.

"Got it, I'll bring more drinks in a bit."

"Okay, where was I—aw, Lahiri--I think Lahiri is my favorite person in their group. We've gotten closest the fastest. She shared with me about her family. It's obvious what they mean to her and how much she misses them. She talked about her culture and their religion. It was apparent how extremely important it all is to her." Delilah scooted in her chair uncomfortably taking a lengthy pause. "But she fell in love with one of her professors here. She feels a lot of shame because her family expected her to keep her virginity until marriage—there was a possibility of an arranged marriage. Lahiri lost the baby. She didn't think she could ever tell her family because she feels it will bring shame on them."

"Whoa, that is rough," I said, typing everything out on Ava's laptop. We had moved the I Spy slides over to her computer while Gemma did her work and while Tabitha was watching what went on with my machine.

"I asked her if she told anyone in the group and she said they all told each other everything. So, I'm assuming that means yes, but she never verified that. The other thing is that Mod's coughing started to get a lot worse, and she is having some stomach issues."

"Really, she thought it was just allergies in the last class," Ava said.

"Well, those are some serious allergies. She looks like death. I told her I would take her to a doctor, but Quinn put the kibosh on that. You know how you get a weird feeling around certain people? He makes me feel very uncomfortable. Mod looked petrified. Oh yeah, and Ava told me you both wanted to know what Mod's locket meant? It's a Kanji symbol for *safety*."

"That seems intense if you feel you have to always wear a locket to feel a sense of safety. I noticed that she fidgets with that locket a lot on screen," Ava said.

I nodded and made note of that. "So, that was the end of the conversation?"

"Nope, he saw how confused I was so he changed his tune to one of fatherly concern saying he had special herbal medicine that he would use to help her. He said he'd monitor the situation and they would take it from there."

"What a prince," I said sarcastically, noting it all.

"I overheard Poppy talking to Linzie about her dream job with a huge production company. She seems particularly driven. I guess Poppy heard that Darla's family was close to some big shots in Hollywood, but later found out it wasn't true. I guess Darla made it all up to get Poppy to do some special costume work for a part she was trying out for. Again, this came from Lahiri."

My head popped up. "She did what? Seriously? That is so mean!"

"That is a pretty crappy thing to do to someone," agreed Gemma.

"Would that make someone angry enough to commit murder?" I wondered.

Our food came out at that moment and many moments of silence persisted as we all stuffed our faces with Carlos—the genius cast iron chef's—magical breakfast skillet meal. The flavors literally popped around in my mouth. I believe we all were moaning at one time or another.

"It's settled, Gemma. We are both selling our businesses and moving here so we can eat here every single day!"

"Agreed. That's a no-brainer!" Gemma beamed patting her stomach and puffing out her cheeks for effect. "I am stuffed!"

"Wow, thanks. I love our business, and making Carlos an assistant manager and giving him more responsibility is one of the best decisions I've ever made!" I grinned.

"Why do you make everything about you, selfish!" Ava declared.

"Girl, behave!" Delilah defended me. I nodded in agreement with her.

"This feels familiar," Gemma said eyeballing Peggy and they shared a laugh.

"Okay, now that I'm stuffed, back to the notes—I'm almost done. Two more things. First, Linzie shared with me that Mod used to be bullied throughout her childhood. I guess because she's so frail and tiny. I don't understand kids sometimes." She looked down, upset at the thought of a child being purposefully hurtful.

"The other thing Linzie told me—well, I asked and she divulged it—was that all of them had a required art course together at the university. Quinn was the TA in the course. He put the group together on a project and worked with them. From there, she said they worked so well together that Quinn talked them into all moving in together to 'keep the band together'—or so he said."

"Geesh, it's so weird how there are people in this world that are so manipulative," Peggy said.

"True, or that so many people can be easily swayed and manipulated," Gemma said.

"Depends on your perspective, I guess," Delilah piped in. "That's all I have."

Meanwhile, the elderly woman that had been sitting so close had gotten up and almost fell into our table reaching for her walker.

"Are you okay?" Ava asked grabbing the walker and helping the lady get situated.

"Thank you, doll—these arthritic legs of mine. So sorry to bother you." She grabbed the check and scooted to the register to pay.

"Well, I have something interesting I found," Gemma said. "I found a chat between Mod and Alyssa. Mod mentioned in the chat that she had been mugged earlier in the week and was having anxiety attacks because of it."

"Mugged?" I said in disbelief. "This must have been after our last class. No one said anything."

"No," Gemma said, "it was during class, see? They sent private chats to each other. They don't come up on the main chat window, but the administrator, which is you guys, can access private chats by going to the chat transcript option. I don't think a lot of people who use this program even know that is an option. And I would guess that Mod and Alyssa had no idea you guys would be able to read them."

"Uh, yeah, that would have been good to know!" I agreed. "I can't believe she got mugged!"

I looked to Delilah, who shook her head sadly. "No one said anything to me. But she looked bad. I thought she had dark bags under her eyes, but now I wonder if it was more than that?"

"Well, there's more. Mod was chatting normally saying 'What if I'm—' then Alyssa cut her off and typed the following," Gemma dug through her stylish artsy bag that I'm sure she bought from Peggy and pulled out a bright green note and handed it to me. Ava looked over my shoulder.

Alyssa: *FHV XLWV*

Mod: *DSZG RU HLNVLMV PMLDH R'N GSV PROOVI?*

"Were you able to decipher what this means?" I asked.

"Not yet, but I'm working on it."

"I don't really have a lot to add, other than the group did show up yesterday afternoon. Mod had what looked like some bruising that may be healing—yellowish around her eyes. The rest of her face was pale, and her body was trembling as she coughed. I offered her some herbal tea and she looked like I offered to kill her."

Lydia walked in, looking around. I waved her over to us.

"What are you doing?" Ava asked.

"Hey, Lydia, can I ask you a medical question?"

Lydia looked suspicious of me. "Okay."

First, I introduced Lydia to Gemma and Peggy letting them know she was a local nurse, then had her pull a chair up to get off her feet and waved over Magda for some tea and donuts, and let her order. I was trying.

"Do you know if seasonal allergies can be so severe that they can cause horrific coughing fits, trembling body, and stomach problems?"

"That is pretty extreme for allergies. I mean, yeah, there are some examples of excessive cases. But if you know of someone who is having those issues then they really should be seeing a doctor immediately. It could also be anxiety—you'd be amazed by how extreme of an effect anxiety can have on a person's physical health."

"Wow, okay, thanks."

"Hey, what's up with you and Nestle anyway?" Ava asked.

I kicked her under the table and gave her a look. She glared at me.

Rubbing her forearms, Lydia exhaled heavily. Next, she fumbled with her cell phone before saying, "He came into the hospital trying to get some information on a patient a couple of weeks ago. I told him it's confidential and refused to share with him. That made him angry."

"Who was the patient?" I asked.

Lydia bit her nails, then pierced me with her green eyes. "I can't tell you that."

Chapter Twelve

I had my hair up, then changed my mind and pulled it down, fluffing it as much as I could. Originally, I had on black capris until I realized they would have cat fur all over them in minutes. I switched to jean capris and my Tom Waits T-shirt and sandals. I didn't want to look too desperate in front of Mick. He was coming over for part two of our conversation, and I was beyond excited.

Doorbell. One more look, a flip of the hair upside down with a quick spray for a fuller look, grabbed the nearest lipstick and flipped it over to see the name of the color—Euro Trash—perfect!

I ran to the door and opened it with a huge smile on my face.

"Well hello, beautiful," he said, pulling a big, colorful bouquet from behind his back.

"Yikes, no one has ever bought me flowers before," I reached for them and inhaled. I was so touched by the sentiment.

"That seems wrong. We need to remedy that," he said, walking past me but not before leaning down, putting his arm around me and kissing me.

This was the life.

"So, I've got a bit of competition, I see," Mick said, reaching down to scratch behind Lenny's ears.

"What? I'm his mama, not his girlfriend," I said giving a little love spanking to Lenny. My cats loved a good tushy patting.

"Not Lenny, Tom," Meiser nodded his head to my T-shirt.

"Nah, you know who Tom Waits is? No way you are that cool!" I teased.

"No way *you* are that cool, young one!"

"I'm an old soul with excellent taste in music."

"I have a surprise for you in the car," Meiser grinned.

"More surprises?"

"Yep, only the best for my girl!" He headed out to his car as I grabbed a vase. I had to hunt for one since it had been so long since I had fresh flowers. I think I may have cut some from the garden at one time way back when.

"Whoa, that's a ton of food," I said, placing the floral arrangement in the middle of the island. I grabbed some plates, napkins, and reached into the fridge for a couple of Cokes.

"It's from the best Italian restaurant in this town."

"So, they opened up a new place?"

Eyebrows raised and he gave me the lengthy detective stare. The one where they fill the room with silence to get the perp to fill the void and confess.

"Kidding," I mumbled.

He laughed.

We sat down to a feast of pizza, calzones, and a yummy Italian sub. I took some of everything. As I shoved food in my face, I noticed Meiser watching me.

"Sorry, I'm hungry. I guess I shouldn't eat like a pig in front of you." I thought back to the book and realized I needed to stop apologizing so much.

"What are you babbling about now, woman? I love the enthusiasm you have for food. I love to watch you eat. You're cute."

"Well then, you will find me to be one of the most adorable people you've ever met."

He reached over and wiped a smear of sauce from my chin and grinned.

"Remember, cute, right?"

He nodded and his eyes turned dark. I started to get that feeling again. Suddenly food wasn't on the front of my mind.

"So, we are doing this, right?" he asked.

"Seems like we are officially doing this . . ." I looked up at him hesitantly. "Could you say what 'this' is, for the record?"

"Sure thing, Counselor," he teased. "We are officially in a relationship. Boyfriend, girlfriend. Yikes. I'm too old for that term. Partners? A couple."

"Soul mates." I made the statement. Whether Mick knew it or not, that was a huge step for me.

"I can agree to that," he held up his Coke can, and we toasted to that.

"So, since we are soul mates now and going to be so honest with each other— "I began.

"I knew it—you women are so wily!"

I ignored that comment, "I met your brother, Miles, at the town meeting last week. He was hanging with Nestle."

"Yeah, those two know each other from way back in the day."

"They do? Is Nestle involved with the mafia? What about Miles? Peggy told me that he had to resign because a man did a blog and reporters started sniffing around—"

"Whoa, we go from soul mates to twenty questions in ten seconds," he said, wide-eyed. "And who is Peggy?"

So far, I wasn't doing so well on this whole adult soul-mate thing. "Right, sorry. Peggy is my friend from Tri-City. She runs Peggy's Pies and Purses on Morrison Ave near the Triopolis campus."

"Oh yeah, I know that area. I've never been there before. I do love a good piece of fig jam pie."

"That does not sound good to me."

"Trust me, when I make you one, you will love it!"

"I have no doubt I'll love whatever you make for me," I got lost in his eyes for several seconds, forgetting where I was going with anything.

"So, more rumors about my family are swirling around, I see." Meiser pulled me out of my reverie.

"I guess. Do you know why your brother resigned?"

"I do. I know we said transparency here, and I understand trust is important in a relationship. There are some things I will not be able to talk about with you if they are ongoing investigations." His tone was very firm.

"You do know that leaves me to make assumptions." Equally firm tone. We were now having a stare-off.

I was the first to cave to fill the silent void—he was really good at this detective stuff. "So, have you heard about how your other brother, Marty, is doing?"

Marty was in jail. There was no doubt he was involved in the mafia, and he had attacked both me and Mick with a knife last Thanksgiving while being involved in other nefarious activities.

"Now, Marty—I can talk about Marty. He's getting by just fine in prison. There are places in this world where being a top guy in the mafia buys you respect. Prison is one of those places. Doesn't mean he wants to stay there, though."

"I'm sorry. I can't imagine all you've been through with your family. It still amazes me to think about how you managed to get out of that life."

We had been sitting in the kitchen chatting after eating and I offered him some coffee while I made myself some tea.

"You know if I'm going to be hanging out more here, then I'm going to need to get us an espresso machine." He sidled up behind me and wrapped his arms around my waist, softly kissing the nape of my neck.

I turned around while in his arms to face him, "I should let you know, when you hold me like this and kiss that spot on my neck, you can pretty much get whatever you want."

"That is great intel to work with." Mick's eyes glowed.

I turned off the tea kettle as my heartbeat

accelerated and my stomach fluttered.

I woke up the next morning with four fluff balls splayed out across me and—I propped up on my elbows and my mouth fell open. That little Sammy Jr. was laying at Mick's feet. He had always been a one-woman cat—a true mama's boy. Furry little traitor!

"Don't tell me you are going to be a handful first thing in the morning too," Meiser said lazily, looking at my expression.

"He's supposed to be a mama's boy." I pointed at Sam splayed across the blanket on top of Mick's legs.

"Yep, still a handful." He reached out and put his arm around me as I snuggled against his side, laying my head on his chest.

"This is nice," I said.

"Very nice. I'm happy we are pursuing this. I hope you know that I'm all in, Jolie. We've both been through a lot in our lives. I feel a strong connection with you."

I looked at him, then kissed him lightly. "I agree. I'm not going to lie. I'm worried. You know I have trust issues. Among other issues."

We both laughed.

"I know that. I hope you don't think I'm holding things back from you because I don't trust you. You know, with some things with my family, because—"

"You don't have to explain. I do understand that with your job, regardless of how much I pry, you can only divulge so much. I promise—I get that."

"I know you can do what you want—go off with your PI bestie and investigate anything you want. I'm not trying to hold you back. It's just that I worry about you getting hurt. Nestle is not a man to mess with. Getting caught up with my family—well, you saw firsthand what that looks like. I couldn't live with it if I was the reason—"

"I get it, Mick, I really do. But here's the thing you need to know—there is an age difference here. And I have no issues with that. But I'm still figuring out a lot of things—trying to understand myself more. I think that's important to do before starting a family." I was lying on his chest and suddenly froze, realizing what I had just said. "Oh, I didn't mean—I just meant—I swear I'm not going there yet—it's just—are you going to let me blabber on forever?"

Mick and I sat up in bed, and he cracked up, "Why yes, I was thoroughly entertained!"

"I'm so happy to amuse you!" I playfully slapped him.

"Hey, our age difference doesn't bother me at all. And all joking aside, the one thing that frightens me in all this is that I do want a family too. As you know, I have MS. That was one of the reasons I was gone for so long. You know I had a flare-up while you were in Santo Domingo. I started a new treatment—it's a trial—in the hopes it will help with my balance issues. I worry about that, or rushing you into something you aren't ready for because I'm older."

"I get it. I think for now we should focus on enjoying the beginning of our relationship and see where it takes us."

"Starting with breakfast?"

I put on my robe and Meiser dressed in yesterday's clothes and we headed down to the kitchen to see what we could make. We walked into the kitchen holding hands to find my Grandma Opal and her beau Tom Costello trying to sneak out the door.

"What in the name of–?" I roared.

Lowering her eyes, Grandma said, "Sorry, I made you a pineapple upside-down cake. I knocked but when you didn't answer, I assumed you two went on a walk for tea so I thought I'd leave it on your island."

Poor Tom clearly felt so awkward he couldn't even raise his eyes to mine. His chin seemed to be glued to his chest.

"Hi, Opal," Mick said, walking to the cake cover and opening it.

Suddenly, my anger dissipated when I saw the caramelized sugar drizzling down the side of the moist cake and the cooked pineapple rings with the bright red cherries in the center of each ring.

"We're sorry," Grandma said, lumping Tom into her bad behavior. "We'll get out of your hair."

Grandma, all four foot nine inches of her, began shoving Tom out the door as he grunted and yelped, "I told you we shouldn't do this!"

"Just go, shush you!"

"And ... that's what it's like to be with me and how my family is—unfortunately," I groaned.

"Well, that's better than them being a mob family."

He made a good point.

I went into the restaurant to do some prepping for the dinner special that night since Ava and I would be doing our last cooking class. I still needed to stop at the store to pick up the ingredients for the skillet chocolate chip cookie. I figured college kids would love it, and it was something I could make in my sleep as often as I made one for myself.

"Wow, you have a glow about you," Ava said, leaning her elbows on the counter with a dreamy look on her face.

"You have got to be kidding me! Grandma is out announcing to the townspeople that I got—"

"What? Grandma Opal caught you doing the nasty?" Ava's beautiful amber skin blanched in disbelief.

"NO! Don't be disgusting!"

"Hey, you may want to take this conversation in the back," Magda's mouth drew into a straight line then she bit her lip.

We looked up and realized that customers were starting to look our way.

I grabbed Ava's elbow and led her through the kitchen where Carlos was cooking.

"She didn't catch us in any act. She dropped a cake off and knocked, when I didn't answer she thought I was out walking with Meiser since his truck was in the drive, so she and Tom used the key—which they were *supposed* to get back to me—to drop off the cake. Oh, hi, Carlos." I smiled awkwardly at him.

"Oh man, this is great stuff," Ava hooted. "You and Meiser finally get it together only for Mama

Opal to come bursting in!"

"I just told you—"

"I leave you two alone for a bit." Carlos nearly sprinted to the front.

I swear Ava and I should have T-shirts made that say *I came. I saw. I made it awkward.*

"If Grandma didn't tell you, then how did you find out?"

"I live next door to you. I saw his truck in the driveway last night and then it was still there this morning. It doesn't take a lot to put it together."

"Oh yeah, that's why my grandma thought we were out walking. That's true. And you are a PI now." I laughed.

"Wow, you are happy—you never let something go this easy. So, how was—"

"Nope, that's as much sharing as this girl is going to do. I'm going to let Carlos know it's safe to leave, and I'll take over and then prep for the dinner crowd later when he comes back."

Later that day, I was getting ready to head out to the store to pick up what we needed when I noticed a pensive look on Ava's face.

"What's wrong?"

"Aren't you worried about tonight? That weirdo, Picasso's whatever said someone wouldn't make it to class tonight."

My elated feelings had put all that out of mind. "That's right. Well, it's almost time for class and we haven't heard anything."

"True. I guess I'll meet you at your house in a little while," Ava pulled at her necklace with a pained expression on her face.

We were all set up and ready to get the last class over with—this entire culinary class project had been so chaotic we were seriously considering making this online cooking course our last one.

We looked at one another and both took a deep breath as the app opened. I made a mental note to make sure everyone was accounted for—except there seemed to be two Lahiri's—Poppy was back at it again. Still, I exhaled when I saw all the faces looked safe and healthy, except Mod's, who had bruises still healing. Since we weren't supposed to know what happened, we acted surprised.

"Oh my gosh, what happened to you?" I asked.

Tad and Quinn stepped into the frame and stood, towering over Mod. Quinn said, "Hey, this is Quinn. Mod was mugged. I've tried to get everyone on board with always being in pairs. We've got each other, so we should be able to always be safe."

Mod looked up from Tad to Quinn with a trembling chin, then went into a coughing fit.

I had had it with these two jerks. I was getting ready to lay into them when Ava pushed her face right up to the computer screen. "Listen up, losers! You are NOT a part of this class. I don't remember seeing any money from either of you. I don't care if you run a cult or not—get your creepy faces off of my screen NOW!"

I could see Tad's cold, flinty eyes go from cocky to angry as his lip curled into a sneer, "This is our home. We have allowed these girls to take this cockamamie cooking class, meaning we are permitting you both into our home. I'd be careful how you speak to us."

I felt a vein protrude in my forehead as red flashed in front of my eyes.

Nostrils flaring, Ava spoke in a voice that shook with fury. "'Allowed,' 'permitted,' oh, you had better be kidding me, man. You want careful? I'll teach you the meaning of carefully smashing your face in you no good little punk—"

Tabitha reached to grab Ava's arm trying to diffuse the situation. The gesture pulled me back to earth. I tried to think of the best way to change the mood when the screen went black.

I looked from Ava to Tabitha, who seemed to be in go-mode, trying to figure what had happened.

"Can they still hear us or see us?" I asked anyone—Bradley or Tabitha.

"Is that weirdo Picasso's Peril coming back?" Ava asked.

"The feed has been cut—they can't see or hear anything. I don't think anyone is coming back on screen," Tabitha said, reaching for her phone. "I'm calling Teddy. I don't like what I saw from them or how terrified that girl looked."

I reached for my phone, too, and called Mick filling him in on what took place and that Tabitha was talking to Teddy.

"Got it, I'm with Teddy. We're heading to the commune now. I'll call you when—"

"We'll see you there," I pressed disconnect looking at Ava as I grabbed my purse. Tabitha had headed out while speaking to Teddy a few minutes ago. Bradley followed behind us.

There was silence the entire thirty-minute drive. I pulled into the gravelly road approaching the cul-de-sac. There were sirens flashing from police vehicles, and two ambulances were on the scene. I felt sick to my stomach. No one moved to get out of the car.

Meiser saw my car and walked toward it with a grim expression.

"Mod's dead."

Chapter Thirteen

I sat at my favorite table at Cast Iron Creations, staring at my laptop screen. There was so much information to process I didn't even know where to start. I glanced down at my notebook, where I had cryptic nonsense written in the margins.

FHV XLWV/DSZG RU HLNVLMV PMLDH R'N GSV PROOVI?

I thought if I stared at the puzzle long enough, the answer would leap out at me. It was clearly some sort of code, but I knew nothing about cryptography. I tried moving some of the letters around, but nothing made any sense.

My thoughts drifted back to the evening before and the task at hand. Teddy, Keith, and Meiser had put up with us wandering around the crime scene for about twenty minutes before they told us in no uncertain terms to leave. We had headed out and pulled out onto the highway, Ava driving while I scribbled down notes of everything we could remember so we could put them into our I Spy Slides.

Because twenty minutes at the crime scene had been plenty.

Now I sat at my restaurant with sheets of scribbled notes spread across the table, trying to remember and make sense of them. Ava was working and it was busy, so she was running around and then dashing over to my table to collaborate when she could. I took a sip from my travel mug of coconut chai and sighed.

Mod. How did I not see it coming? She had been covered in bruises, terrified. It was so obvious something was very wrong. Last night at the commune, Meiser disappeared inside The Magic Cave with a forensic kit to process the scene while Keith wound police tape around the second Victorian house on that street in a month's time. Meanwhile, Teddy corralled all the residents of the commune for questioning. Quinn and Tad were downright hostile, questioning the police at every turn.

Ava and I inched over by the group of residents they were collecting statements from. They stood stiffly, Quinn and Tad positioned themselves between the group and anyone who approached. Teddy pulled Linzie first. He walked her over near his cruiser and started asking her questions.

"Who was the last person to see Mod alive?" I demanded to the group once he was out of earshot. I had to swivel around to make eye contact with all of them because of Tad and Quinn blocking us. "How was she? Did anyone actually see her die?"

"After the session ended, we all decided to go watch TV in The Magic Cave," Lahiri murmured. Her eyes were red from crying. "Mod said she didn't feel well, so she went to her room to lie

down. She died alone in her room. Allison found her."

"Um, are you Lahiri or Poppy?" I had to ask. She reached up and pulled a wig off, then wiped a swipe of makeup off of her cheek—part of the real Poppy appeared. It freaked me out completely.

"We don't know how she died, if that is your next question," snapped Quinn. He was about the same height as Tad, raven-haired and square-jawed, with luminous blue eyes. It was easy to see how young, impressionable students, particularly females, might be influenced by his charisma.

"Hey," said Ava loudly, "can any of you tell me where Mod was when she was mugged?"

The students shifted uncomfortably behind the two tall boys.

"She was on the Triopolis U campus, walking to her car after class." growled Tad. "Some jerk grabbed her and hit her and took her bag. We'll find out who it was and take care of it."

"What does that mean, 'take care of it'?" I asked. Tad didn't respond. "Where were all of you on the night Mod was mugged?" Quinn gritted his teeth. "We don't have to answer your questions," he snarled. "Mod was one of us. We would never hurt her."

Teddy must have been finished with Linzie, because she came back, and Teddy motioned for Lahiri to follow him.

"I'm not sure why you're asking us all of this," said wide-eyed Allison. "Tad and Quinn wouldn't hurt any of us. Quinn is the one who brought us all together." She gazed at him with adoration. "He is our mentor. He takes care of us. He blended a special herbal tea to help Mod heal after her *attack."*

"See?" Quinn smirked, "none of her friends harmed her. Mod wasn't well. Maybe she died of natural causes." Lahiri and Teddy came over from the police cruiser. Lahiri rejoined the group and Teddy tapped Allison. He had almost walked away again when he reeled around glared at Ava and me.

"You ladies shouldn't be here, this is a crime scene," he chided.

"Okay, we were just going," I promised. I hated to lie to Teddy. "We're so sorry for your loss," I said to the group, then we headed for the car. I had been met with red eyes from everyone except Tad and Quinn, who fixed me with a challenging stare.

"I almost offered to refill your coffee," laughed Ava, startling me out of my reverie by appearing at my table, hoisting a coffee carafe. "But then I remembered you are nuts about tea. Let me put this back and I think I can sit down for a second."

She plopped down a few seconds later. "Did you get everything put into I Spy Slides?"

"Yes, I think so. Everyone told us where they were when Mod was being mugged, but there isn't any proof. Same for when she died. They claim Mod was alone in her room and Allison found her. They don't know cause of death yet. Tad and Quinn are massive creepazoids. Did I forget anything?"

Ava growled. "Nothing fires me up like men who think they can tell women what to do. Those two ordering the women in that commune around—it makes me sick!"

"I know that communes and cults aren't the same thing, but those guys really come off like cult leaders, especially Quinn," I commented. "They seem to give in to whatever he says without question."

"I know, it is really eerie," agreed Ava. She looked over my shoulder and her eyebrows shot up. She stood up quickly. "Okay, better check my tables again," she said as she rushed away. *What on earth?*

I turned to see Meiser pushing the door of the restaurant open. My heart immediately began to flutter. He looked at Mirabelle, who pointed at me. He turned and sauntered in my direction. I could feel my face flushing. I felt like everyone in the restaurant had either heard about our steamy encounter, or they could read it in print on my burning face. He sat down across from me.

"Hello, sweetie." He smiled, then quirked an eyebrow. "I can't believe you came to the crime scene yesterday. I feel like you have literally no respect for police procedure, my dear."

I managed a shrug. "There's a bet in the works. I can't lose ground on the case. I'll crack this one first, mark my words."

Meiser sighed. "I hope someone will. I haven't come across one this weird in a long time." His phone rang. He stood and walked a few paces from the table. I put my headphones in so I could concentrate on my work as he talked. My media player crashed, and as I waited for it to restart, Meiser paced close to me, talking on the phone.

"Thanks, Colleen, yeah." *The coroner! Was this the autopsy report?* "Heart failure? Yes. Tox screen? What? Spell it. D-A-P-H-N-E-T-I-N. Okay. Was it cause of death? Okay. Thanks. Yeah, that's probable cause for Kingsley. We're going to bring him in. Yeah. Bye."

I felt slightly guilty, but I quickly wrote down everything I had overheard anyway, then put on an innocent expression just as he sat back down across from me.

"What's up?" I asked. He grabbed my hand and kissed the middle knuckle.

"Why do we always have to meet like this?" he asked softly. "I have to get going. When can I see you again?"

"As soon as humanly possible," I said, squeezing his hand. "Text me when you get off of work and we'll plan something."

"That sounds just delicious." He gave one last smoldering look and left.

I shook myself out of the rosy daydream I was in and turned to my laptop, typing "daphnetin" into my search bar.

A toxin occurring naturally in the berries of the Daphne bush. Okay, Daphne bush. Grows in this region. Toxic to dogs and humans. Symptoms, irritation of throat and skin. *The coughing and blotchy face.* Gastric distress. *Stomach problems!* Cardiac arrhythmia. Death. *Yes, that fit the bill. Poor Mod.* I was sure that Quinn had put the berries in the tea he made for Mod.

I was taking notes on poison derived from plants when the door opened and my Aunt Fern came into the restaurant with the mayor right behind her. Mirabelle seated them and I could see them talking for a moment before Aunt Fern excused herself to come over to me.

"Did you see I am here with Fitan?" Aunt Fern looked giddy. I had never heard anyone call our mayor by his first name before. "Isn't he handsome? I've had a crush on him for years. He was the secret admirer I told you about. This is our third date!"

"Aw, Aunt Fern, that's sweet! I'm glad you two found each other."

"Yeah, sorry I never texted you back. It got late and I thought you'd be asleep, and then it slipped my mind."

I didn't ask for any details of that story, but congratulated her again and encouraged her to try today's special, then I went back to my table to continue my research.

A few hours later, I was back home, sitting on the couch. I realized that Lenny was buzzing. He looked annoyed, but not annoyed enough to move. He buzzed again. "Lenny, are you sitting on my phone?" I cooed.

"Meooowwww," Lenny replied non-committally. I lifted him gently and grabbed my phone. Three messages from Tink.

Hey, you busy?

I have a question.

I need to show you something. Can I come over?

Are you okay? Of course, come on over, I texted back. Ten minutes later, there was a knock at my door and I opened it to find my young cousin with his strawberry blonde floppy hair, freckles, and that ornery grin permanently plastered on his face standing in my doorframe. He walked in and tossed a baggie on my kitchen table.

"I was walking the dog out in the fields by the

Italian restaurant, you know, where those holes are?" Tink said. "I wasn't looking for nothin, not really, but I came across these patches of this dark oily liquid in the dirt. So I started poking around with my foot and I found these caps. Look. Tell me what you think." He pushed the bag toward me.

I picked it up and looked at it. Three metal screw-on caps that looked like they fit bottles. *Weird. What was this doing out in a field? It looks like cooking oil.*

"Great find, Tink." I smiled at him. "Do you care if I hang onto this?"

Tink looked pleased that I thought it was important. "Sure, maybe show it to that cop guy you are ..." he blushed, "hanging out with."

I chuckled. *Maybe I will.*

"Okay, I gotta go," Tink said. "Will you text me if you find out anything interesting about those caps?"

"Promise I will." I smiled at him. "Thanks for showing me. Great detective work!"

As soon as the door closed behind him, I hustled to the bathroom. I studied my reflection, adding a bit of mascara for good measure, running my fingers through my curly hair. I needed to look my best. I needed to talk to Meiser.

I opened the front door of M&M, Leavensport's Italian restaurant, owned by Meiser himself. The food was exquisite, but I was in pursuit of something else. The first person I came across was Bea, who was working the front of the house.

"Jolie! How are you?" Bea bubbled, in full-on hospitality mode. "How many will you be dining with?"

"Actually, Mrs. Seevers, I am looking for Mick. Is he in?"

"Last time I saw him, he was in the back, but he might have left. Should I go check for you?"

"Yes, in a second. But, how are you? It seems like this place has turned out to be a good fit for you."

"Oh, yes, I like it a lot. Mick just promoted me to assistant manager. I run the front of the house now. The money is actually quite good." Bea smiled proudly. "We were hurting financially there for a while, but now it is smooth sailing."

"Oh, wow, that is marvelous! Well, you earned it. This place seems like it is running like a machine."

"I had a little bit of extra money lately, so I got some of that Lasik surgery, with the lasers?" Bea leaned in like she was telling me a secret while batting her blue eyes at me. "I was embarrassed about my old lady glasses, so I thought I would get that surgery. Earl is away fishing with his buddies, and when he gets back, I won't have glasses. It's a surprise."

My jaw dropped. Everything fell into place. "Is that why you had those sunglasses on the other day?" I asked.

"Yeah, I didn't really want to blab it all over town. Old lady surgery."

I giggled. "I don't think Lasik is really old lady surgery, but you look great without your glasses!" I needed to revise my I Spy Slides entry on Bea Seevers as soon as humanly possible.

"Thanks, Jolie. Do you want to go back there yourself and check if Mick is here?" She looked coyly at me. "I'm sure he'd be happy to see you."

I blushed and hurried through the dining room to the back. Meiser was sitting in the back office, looking over some paperwork. He glanced up and grinned.

"I wasn't expecting to see something so lovely in my office. What can I do for you?" he grabbed my wrists and kissed my palms. My body flooded with warmth, and I almost forgot why I was there.

I shook myself. "Tink found something in the field. I want you to look at it." I pulled the baggie out of my leather bag and handed it to him. "Maybe you can make some sense of why there would be oily caps in a field."

Meiser opened the bag and smelled the contents. He put a latex glove on and pulled a cap out, looking at it closely. He swiped some of the oily substance off, rubbing it between his fingers.

"Well," he concluded, putting the cap back in the bag and closing it carefully, then stripping off the glove. "These caps usually go on olive oil bottles. And this looks like premium oil, imported, I would guess. This is interesting. Very interesting. Olive oil." He rubbed his chin and looked lost in thought.

Then he turned to me. "This is a great find. Thank you." I nodded, accepting the compliment. He stepped closer, enclosing me in his arms. "You're really talented at this, you know." He leaned in and gave me a long, deep kiss. My knees were weak. I shook my head to clear it.

"Did you just admit I'm better than you at detective work?" I gave a sideways smile.

"Never!"

"Well, for the good of all, I will catch you up on your murder case ..."

"Oh yeah?" His eyebrow quirked. "Well, I can't tell you everything, but I welcome any information you can bring to the table."

"I can work with that," I nodded. "Let me tell you what I know that you probably don't. First, Tad was cheating on his girlfriend, Alyssa, with our first murder victim, and before her death she tried to pressure him to end things with Alyssa." Meiser's eyebrows shot up.

I continued. "Also worth noting, Darla lied to Poppy, telling her that she had connections in Hollywood in order to get her to make a costume for her." Meiser sat heavily down into the office chair, his jaw slack with surprise.

I kept going. "Mod has looked frightened and ill for the past week, and admitted that she had been mugged a week ago. Quinn stated that she was mugged in a parking lot on Triopolis U campus, but no one else can corroborate that story."

"Wow," Meiser said in awe. "That is really helpful."

"Well?" I replied proudly, "what can you tell me? Have you taken Quinn into custody?"

"Yes, and we can hold him for twenty-four hours. For a while we thought it was Tad, but we couldn't come up with enough evidence to bring him in. Mod died of heart failure from poisoning, her tox screen came up positive for plant compound called daphnetin. We think Quinn was slipping it to her somehow, tinkering around with how much it would take to kill her. He had a knowledge of herbs and various local plants and their properties."

"Tea. He was dosing her tea. She mentioned that Quinn was making her herbal tea to help her feel better. And here I thought she had allergies and maybe some stomach issues. Poor girl."

"Well the information that you have provided gives us a much clearer picture of what is going on over there."

"Is it possible that they are all in on it in some way?" I asked.

"It is definitely possible."

"The way Tad and Quinn treated those women, like they were soldiers, telling them what to think and do. It gave me the creeps. In class, Mod seemed terrified of both of them. And Tad is still over there. They're still in danger!"

Meiser's brow furrowed. "Don't do anything crazy, you have to stay safe."

"I won't, if you promise me you'll keep an eye on them. I need to know you have a plan."

"Please just stay away and stay safe. We'll take care of it." He stood up and leaned over, kissing me on the forehead.

Chapter Fourteen

Peggy, Ava, Delilah, and I were gathered in my living room. We had decided something needed to be done to keep the remaining members of the art commune safe.

Peggy put her phone in her pocket. "Gemma just drove by the commune. Tad's car is gone."

"Perfect!" crowed Ava. "Now is the time to strike. Call over there, tell them to pack up and head for the B&B. I have a luxury family suite reserved with three queen beds. That is plenty of room for all of them."

"Yeah, we need to hurry," I added nervously. "We don't know when he is coming back, and also, Quinn will get released in the next few hours if Teddy and Meiser can't find enough evidence to hold him."

"We have to keep them calm, but get them out of there," urged Delilah. "We should call one of them and tell them the plan. Also, I doubt this is legal, but I have those small little security cameras that I keep at the gallery. I'd feel better about putting one somewhere in their room—they have the family room and kitchen area in the suites—there is no audio but then we could use our phones to check in on them to make sure they are safe—what does everyone think? I can run over there right now and do it since we paid for the suite. The footage goes to a website we can access from our phones so we can check it any time."

Ava put her hands up in caution. "Okay, hold on a second. Putting a camera inside a hotel room is really illegal."

"So we shouldn't?" asked Delilah.

Ava took a breath and thought about it for a moment. "I don't know. Our safety might be worth it. But we would have to swear to keep this a secret. I could lose my PI license over this."

We all looked at one another.

"Also, if we did see anything on the camera, it would be inadmissible as evidence in a court of law. It wouldn't help put the killer behind bars."

We sat quietly for a moment, weighing the costs and benefits.

"I say go for it," Peggy said. I nodded.

"I'll install it once we're finished here," Delilah said.

"We have Alyssa, Poppy, and Lahiri's phone numbers from the class application form. Which one of them are we going to call?" wondered Ava.

"I'd call Alyssa," I said.

"No way!" said Ava. "She's out of the running in my book. That stunt she pulled the first day of class was immature. She can't be trusted. And Poppy's compromised because of the whole thing with Darla. I vote Lahiri." She crossed her arms over her ample bosom and stuck her chin out at me.

"I have to agree with Ava," Delilah said. "I have hung out at that place a lot, and Lahiri is a really sincere, sweet kid who wants what is best for the group. She's the one."

"No," I persisted. "Alyssa is trustworthy. I really think it was Tad's fault. We all know how he is. And she is already not happy with him. I get the feeling she had some idea about the affair. She probably doesn't really trust him."

"I'm sure she's trustworthy," agreed Peggy.

At this, Ava nodded in reluctant agreement.

Delilah shrugged. "Okay, let's give Alyssa a call. I'm heading to the B&B now to get the camera in place."

I dialed her number. She picked up almost immediately. "Hey Alyssa. Ava and Deh—" I stopped myself, "and Peggy and Gemma, the women from the shops, and I are worried about you. There's something we have to tell you that might be difficult to hear." I took a deep breath. "We think Quinn and Tad might be in on the murders together."

I let a few beats of silence pass to allow her to process this news. This was her boyfriend, after all. "We're worried you are in danger if you stay at that house. We want to put all of the girls up in the bed and breakfast in Leavensport for a few nights to keep you safe. How does that sound?"

"Tad? You think Tad?" she stuttered. "He can be a jerk and an idiot sometimes, but ... all of this? No way."

"Are you sure?" I asked gently. "Hasn't he been acting strange lately? In your heart, don't you know that something isn't quite right?" Alyssa fell silent. I could hear her breathing on the line.

"I don't know anything right now," she said finally. "But what you're saying makes some sense." She sighed. "And if you're right and more of my friends get hurt or killed because I couldn't swallow my pride and see things for how they really are ... okay. Tell me the plan." Alyssa agreed, telling me that she would talk to the group and text us back soon.

Forty-five minutes later, I pulled into the parking lot of Make Yourself at Home Bed and Breakfast. I saw the ladies from the commune getting out of a car and pulled in next to them. Ava was in the car with me, but Delilah was in Dee mode, and had driven separately to get the camera set up, and with the plan of staying in the room with the girls in order to keep a close eye on them.

We all stood in the parking lot for a moment. It had begun to drizzle and everyone seemed crabby. Who could blame them? This whole thing was awful.

Delilah got out and popped her trunk, pulling out her duffel bag and looping it over her shoulder. "Hi guys, I heard what happened. I can't believe Mod is gone." Delilah's eyes filled with real tears. "Anyway, I was hoping I could stay over here with you since the house is ... you know ... the danger zone."

"Um, how did you say you knew we were over here, at this bed and breakfast?" Alyssa's voice was sharp and her brow furrowed.

Delilah blanched at the cross-examination. "I ... uh ... drove by the house and ran into ... the police guy, what's his name?" she stuttered unconvincingly. "He said you were staying here. For safety." She looked flustered.

"Speaking of the house," I said, trying to distract everyone, "are Linzie and Allison on their way?"

"No, they aren't coming," Lahiri said. "They refuse to believe that either Tad or Quinn could have anything to do with the murders and insist that they are perfectly safe at the commune. We tried and tried but they won't give in. They're staying there."

I shook my head and sighed, then pulled my phone out and texted Teddy, telling him the plan and the fact that there were two girls staying behind at the commune, asking if he could send a patrol car around every few hours to check on them. Tad would be back soon, and Quinn would be a free man in just a few hours unless the police could find some reason to keep him. I shuddered at the thought.

Ava, Peggy, Gemma, and I all helped the girls with their bags, and we checked them in. We took the stairs up to the second floor of the charming bed and breakfast to find the three-bedroom suite. Since Linzie and Allison wouldn't be there, there was plenty of room, even with the addition of Dee.

"Wow," gushed Lahiri, "this place is really nice!" The girls threw their bags down and began exploring. The rooms had a Medieval feel with tapestries on the walls and arched doors and windows matching the castle design of the building.

I excused myself and went into the restroom. I washed my hands, checking my hair in the mirror. I felt better knowing that at least these three girls were safe. I tried not to think too hard about Linzie and Allison. As I turned to go back out into the suite, I tripped over someone's bag on the floor, launching the contents across the tile.

I gasped. The mask! Tangled in a pile of socks and T-shirts was the upside-down mask! Whose bag was this? I dug through it. It was all pretty common stuff. A few medium shirts, a few large, some one-size-fits-all pajamas. This bag could belong to any of the girls out there.

Which meant one of them was Picasso's Peril. One of them was behind all of this. Or was covering for the killer? Or the killer slipped the mask in her bag? My mind immediately leaped to Tad and Quinn.

I suddenly sensed that I had been in the bathroom for too long. I pulled my phone out and quickly texted Delilah. *Make an excuse. You can't stay here tonight. I'll explain later. We have to go.*

When I emerged, the girls were talking casually about room service, deciding what to order for dinner. Delilah's eyebrows were high on her forehead. She grabbed her phone.

"Oh! That's unexpected. My aunt just texted and said my cousin is in town tonight," Delilah ad-libbed. "I haven't seen her in years. I should probably go."

"Oh," Alyssa said icily, "yes, you probably should."

"Dee" gave Lahiri a quick hug and grabbed her duffel bag.

"Yeah, we ought to head out, too," I agreed. "So, you gals are good to stay here until everything calms down?"

"Yes, and thanks so much for getting us these rooms," Poppy said, smiling. "I feel much safer now."

"Okay, text us if anything crazy happens," I reminded them.

Ava, Delilah, Peggy, Gemma, and I headed down the stairs. Once we hit the parking lot, the other four reeled on me.

"What the heck was that? Spill!" demanded Ava.

"We need to get back and add to our I Spy Slides—also, it was smart to put that camera in there—we need to keep an eye on them tonight," I said, my voice shaking. "We were completely wrong. One of them is in on it. I don't know who. Look what I found." I opened my bag and showed them the upside-down mask.

"Hey, how is that four-top coming along?" Ava yelled into the kitchen.

I shook myself. I had been in dreamland the entire shift. I plated the dishes and transferred them to a big tray, dinging the bell to signal to Ava that they were ready to go.

I knew in my heart, for the safety of the people of Leavensport, that I needed to tell the police—preferably Meiser, preferably in person, and preferably with his arms around me—what I knew about the mask.

Unfortunately, I got up late and barely made it to work on time. Then it happened to be one of the busier days I had ever worked, and I hadn't even had time to think about it, let alone confer with Ava on what our plan of action ought to be. She wasn't exactly level-headed either, running around with trays, her eyes wild and her hair getting puffier by the minute.

But shifts end, as they always do. I will admit that Carlos' silhouette in the doorway of the kitchen was the most beautiful thing I had ever seen. We exchanged pleasantries as I did the last few dishes, and I headed out.

Ava and I walked home together. She turned to me when we got to her door. "Are you going to call him?" she asked.

"As soon as I get inside," I assured her. "Did the commune girls contact you?"

"Nope."

"Me either."

"Okay, get some rest. Message me if anything changes."

"Will do."

I unlocked my door and was met by hungry cats. I fed them and petted them, then dug my phone out. I checked the camera at the B&B. They were just doing normal things, sleeping, watching TV.

Are you busy? I have something you need to see, I messaged Meiser.

Less than a minute later: *What is it? Can I come over?*

Please do.

Fifteen minutes later, I heard a knock on my door. It was just long enough for me to change my shirt, fluff my hair, and brush my teeth. Just in case. You never knew.

"What's up?" He scooped me into his arms as he asked. I melted into them, struggling to remember why I had called him over in the first place. He pulled himself out of the embrace first.

"What did you want to tell me?" he asked. I

shook myself. "You first. What have you found on Quinn?"

"That kid." Meiser shook his head. "That kid is slick. We searched the whole commune, all three houses. We took fingerprints, a ton of samples. We even found the famous herbal tea that he was giving Mod. Nothing. No berries, no toxin. No evidence."

"Nothing at all?"

"Nope. I mean, there are definitely Daphne bushes growing in the area, but nothing in the house. Not a trace."

"Do you think he didn't do it?"

"No, I think he did it, I just think he is really good at cleaning up after himself."

"Pretty smart," I mused.

"Actually, after having talked to him, I don't think he really is. His family has a lot of money, that's for sure. They already have a high-priced lawyer skulking around. Honestly, he comes off as an uneducated, entitled, spoiled little brat. He is good with his hands, though. He has an iron forge in that little shed next to the house at the commune, did you know that?"

"Someone said something about it, but I didn't get a chance to actually to look at it."

"Yeah, he made that iron sign at the entrance to the commune."

"Wait," I gasped. "The murder weapon! An iron stake! I bet Quinn made it!"

Meiser sighed heavily. "Yeah, he made it. Admitted it from the beginning. It was part of a new sign he was working on. He showed me the plans."

"That sounds pretty smart to me."

"It just sounds like he thought it through,"

Meiser grumbled. "Anyway, he said someone took it from his room the day of the murder. He said his fingerprints would be all over it."

"Perfect cover story," I muttered.

"It really is," agreed Meiser. "Although we checked the stake for prints and it was wiped clean."

"I wonder why he bothered admitting it, then?"

"Who knows?"

"Maybe he knew you'd find out eventually and wanted to get ahead of it." I theorized.

Meiser shrugged. "All I know is, Teddy runs that department, and his brain is powered by facts, not hunches. You won't get anywhere on a gut feeling with that man. That is part of why he and Tabitha don't always see eye to eye. She has worked with people, been a therapist, seen inside people's minds, besides working for the FBI. She gets feelings about people based on their behavior. She looks at the psychology behind it all."

"And what is her hunch about that group?" I asked, already halfway knowing the answer.

"That there is a kingpin, a manipulator in the group, moving pieces around on a chess board. Probably Quinn, maybe Tad." *Couldn't agree more.* "What did you want to tell me?"

"Two things." I looked at him nervously. "The first thing you aren't going to like."

"Well?"

"Um, well, we put a camera in their hotel room—FOR SAFETY—" I said, seeing the expression on his face. "And it's a good thing we did."

Meiser took the longest, slowest breath I have ever heard.

"Do you have any idea how illegal–" He stopped for another extremely long breath. *Good heavens, this man must love oxygen.* "Just ... why on earth ... would you do that?"

"Because of the second thing I wanted to tell you!" I said brightly. "I found this in one of the girl's bags at the hotel room." I pulled the mask out of my bag.

I thought Meiser's jaw was going to keep dropping until it hit the floor.

"Locating that has been at the top of the priority list since day one," he whispered. "and you found it. Where was it?"

"In one of the girls' bags," I replied. "I have no idea whose, the contents were pretty bland."

"But it was either Poppy, Alyssa, or Lahiri," he confirmed. He pulled out his phone.

"One of those three."

"Okay. Here's what I'm going to do. I'm going to add that camera to the search warrant. It's called a sneak-and-peek. But this is between you and me, because warrants are supposed to be in place," –he glared at me–"*before* the camera is installed."

"Yes, sir," I said meekly.

He stared hard at me for three or four seconds. Then he walked slowly toward me and put his hands around my waist. He leaned toward me and kissed me hard.

"Whew!" I said, fanning myself. "At least I know how to get you going—hand you clues on a murder case."

Meiser cracked up laughing. He was so hot when he laughed. His brown eyes crinkled up and he flashed a brilliant, sultry smile. "Of course, you know that we won't be able to pull a fingerprint off of that mask, since you and everyone you have ever met has touched it."

"Yeah, I know." I arched an eyebrow at him. "Coming up with an excuse for losing already?"

"Oh, are we still doing that? I had forgotten."

"You can't back out now, 'The game is afoot!'" I quoted my favorite mystery author.

"So, if you find the culprit first ..." He nuzzled my neck. I closed my eyes.

"I ... choose the prize ..."

"And if I win, I choose the prize?" he murmured into my hair.

"Sure ..." I whispered, forgetting what I was agreeing to.

Chapter Fifteen

The next morning, Ava burst into the kitchen with a look of eager expectation.

"What is wrong with you?"

"So, I saw the Meisermobile in the drive last night, but not this morning. Are you two off again or what's going on?"

"We are fine. Actually, we are more than fine," I waggled my eyebrows and Ava made a gag me gesture. "You asked!"

Ava laughed it off.

I continued to fill Ava in on everything Mick had shared with me last night about holding Quinn for twenty-four hours, but Tad was out.

"I did give him the mask I found. I can't hinder a police investigation to win a bet," I said as Ava looked at me like I was nuts.

"So, the challenge is still on—but, he has an unfair advantage. You need to remind him of that!"

"What's that?"

"You're his girlfriend now. Like the mask—you

said it, you had to give it to him. That should work in your favor. Also, you have a best friend who is the number one private investigator in Leavensport."

"I don't think there are any—"

"Not the point!" Ava stabbed a finger at me.

"Got it," I said hands splayed in the air. "Hey, I've been meaning to ask you. Do you have both of our cast-iron skillet lockets? I was going to wear mine the other day, but I can't find it anywhere?"

"I don't think I would have yours. I remember you wore it the night Darla was murdered. You hadn't worn it the first class, and you made a big stink about how cool it would be if we both wore ours. So, I did too."

"That's right. I always take it off before I go to bed. I wonder if it fell off when we went to the compound or at the police station? I'll have to ask Teddy, but I will not be asking Tad or Quinn."

"I'll text Delilah and have her keep her eyes open for it."

"Thanks, I appreciate that. Well, I don't know about you, but I give up on these online cooking classes—at least with this group."

"Agreed. Maybe we'll try again around the holidays this year, BUT I do not want to do this with college students again. I think we should try it with people here in Leavensport again."

We had run a couple of free pilot courses with people from the town in preparation for those that paid. Then we scaffolded even more by making the first round of paid clients have a discount since we were new to it.

"I don't know. We did that with the testing.

Maybe we'll ask around in the restaurant or maybe we'll see if Peggy knows some people interested from the city. Opening it up to anyone again makes me nervous."

"Yep, those college kids have traumatized me for life! Since we worked double shifts yesterday to get today off, do you think we should watch the recordings of the class again to see if we can find anything. I mean, we want to make sure you win this bet."

"You load it on your computer. I'm too paranoid after Tabitha had my computer."

"Did she or Meiser ever say anything about noticing what you were looking up? Gemma seemed like she knew what she was doing—but finding that private chat and the code told us a lot."

"Nope, and honestly, I don't feel like either of them have acted awkward or suspicious. I'm not tech-savvy, nor do I know anything about legalities. Maybe legally they can only focus on things tied directly to the investigation?"

"That's a good point. Besides, it's yours and you are helping them. So, even if they did look—they really shouldn't have been. I'm going to run over and grab my laptop. Be back in a flash."

I was feeling extremely guilty about all the things I was doing behind Ava's back. I know there was nothing horrible but working closely with Delilah trying to find out more about Nestle—plus, knowing something that Ava doesn't know. That had become our thing the last couple of years—investigating things together.

I decided it was time to end this but I didn't want to ambush Delilah, so I texted her.

Hey, I'm so sorry, but I am feeling horrible

about keeping this from Ava. I can't keep doing this.

Ava popped back in and was setting up her laptop sitting at the island with me when my phone dinged.

"Who's that?" She asked.

"Delilah, she's on her way here."

"Why?"

"Let's just start the recordings and look over them. We'll all talk when she gets here."

Ava gave me a quizzical look.

She fired up the first recording and we both watched about fifteen minutes of footage before stopping to discuss what we saw.

"I'm going to note things they are wearing, if anyone is acting awkward or afraid—" I grabbed my notebook.

"Add in what the backgrounds look like from one recording to another. We have to remember that they are all into some sort of art—special effects, acting, graphic design—if there are any of them that are great with computers, who knows what is real and what is fake."

"Good point. If we make a bunch of notes from the recordings, we can come back to them to cross-reference."

The doorbell rang. I took a deep breath, wondering how all this would go.

"Hey, Jolie," Bradley said.

"Oh, hey, Bradley. I thought you were going to be someone else."

"Your new boyfriend?" Bradley grinned.

Ava walked into the living room, laughing. "So

the whole town knows?"

"Of course, they do!" Bradley said.

"What about you and Betsy? Are you two a hot item now?" I teased back.

"I don't think that is going to work. I don't know—I think I was hurt more than I thought about Lydia and Keith. Plus, I know Betsy has a thing for Teddy. We went out. It was nice, don't get me wrong. There wasn't a connection."

"Way to put your foot in your mouth again, Tucker," Ava said.

"I don't think you are one to give her crap about my relationships, Ava," Bradley gave her a wry grin.

I was happy the two of them could finally joke about their past and his sister Delilah being the one for Ava.

There was a knock at the door.

"You should get that," I said looking at Bradley and nodding at the door.

He made an odd face and opened the door, "Hey sis, how's it going?"

Delilah looked pleasantly surprised and grabbed her big brother giving him a bear hug. "Long time, no see."

"I don't want to keep anyone. I just popped over to see what was going on with the classes?" Bradley asked.

"Over and done for now," Ava said.

I put my index finger up signaling him to hold on and went for my checkbook.

"What are you doing?" Bradley asked.

"Writing you a check for what we agreed to pay

you," I said while making it out.

"Don't worry about it. I already had all the equipment, and it was all such a disaster."

"I know. We are talking about refunding everyone's money," Ava said.

"Then definitely do not pay me," Bradley waved off the check I was holding out to him.

"Are you sure? We can just eat the money," I said.

"Nah, I'm okay. I'll have lots more money anyway now that I've given up on love."

"What? You're a catch. You can't give up," Delilah gave him a light punch to the biceps.

"Hey, while you are here, are you willing to take a look at something for us that our friend Gemma found?" I asked thinking about the weird code.

"Sure thing, who is Gemma?"

"She's a lady that runs a jewelry shop in Tri-City. She's a computer whiz like you," I said wondering if I should try to fix those two up. I am already juggling so much. Why do I always get myself into more trouble?

I grabbed the code and showed him and explained as best I could what Gemma had done.

"Oh, I'll bet she used an mSpy chat tracker once she knew the phone numbers—which is easy to find on the internet," Bradley said.

I stared at him like a deer in the headlights. "Mmmmkay, anyway, here's the code. I haven't heard back from her yet, so I'm assuming she hasn't broken the code."

"Ooooh, a challenge! Can I take your computer up to your office really quick to take a look at a few things?"

"Sure thing. You know Tabitha had—"

"I'm not worried about it. No one will know what I'm doing."

People are pretty shady when it comes to technology. Note to self: always think about what you do and say on the computer.

"What are you two up to?" Delilah asked after Bradley ran upstairs.

"Watching recordings to see if we can find anything that is off. You should help us since you have been the one hanging out with them the most," Ava said, oblivious that we were about to wreck her world.

"Sure," Delilah said, looking at me sideways.

I got the feeling she was in no rush to tell Ava what was going on.

We continued to watch the recordings, stopping to discuss and take notes. Bradley must have got lost in his technical world because we hadn't seen or heard from him. An hour passed and we started the next recording and were about ten minutes in when Delilah yelled, "STOP—Go back."

Ava rewound the recording.

"Okay, stop. Now can you split screen it and look at the last recording of Mod?"

Ava and I looked at each other and both put our palms up in the air and shrugged.

"Bradley!" Delilah yelled up to her brother.

Bradley came down, and Delilah told him what she wanted. Within less than a minute he had it done.

"Look," Delilah pointed at Mod from one frame

to the next.

"Uh, what am I looking at?" I squinted.

"Oh yeah, great catch, sis," Bradley said bending over top of where I was sitting to point. "See, Mod is standing by Alyssa in each frame. "She's taller than her in this one—"

"Oh my gosh, and way shorter than her in this one," Ava said looking at me.

"Stilts of some sort?" I asked, looking from one face to the next.

"That would be my guess. Drywall stilts wrap around your calf, and if she practiced, she could walk in them pretty smoothly. But I have no idea why would she need or want to be taller. Hey, I should have something figured out for you soon on that code. I'm heading back up."

"Wow, this is crazy. But Mod is dead. It seems like she was playing a significant role in all of this, but now she's dead?" Ava speculated.

"That could be a good motive to kill her. You saw how nervous she was. Someone was afraid she would talk," I said.

"Um, Ava, can we change the subject for a minute?" Delilah had picked D.J. up and was stroking her fur.

"Sure, what's up?" Ava typed a few things into the I Spy Slides.

Sweat began to form on my palms. I rubbed my hands up and down on my jeans.

"Uh-oh," Ava was watching my hands. She knew me too well.

"Delilah and I have been keeping something from you that we need to tell you," I said.

Ava's   head   flinched   back   slightly   in

uncertainty. "What's going on?"

"First off, Jolie is not to blame. I'm the one who got her involved in all this—" Delilah started.

Poking her tongue into her cheek and inhaling a long breath, Ava said, "Would you both stop ho-humming around and tell me what is happening before I start making assumptions that the two of you are having an affair?"

My eyes began to rapidly blink willing Delilah to get on with it.

"Right, it's not that, of course," I said.

"Sweetie, listen, when everything was going down with your family last February, I needed a way to come up with more money. I sold part of my shares of the gallery. Your dad gave me the money back, and I tried to buy the shares back, but the buyer refuses to sell back to me. That's it. I enlisted Jolie's help to help me figure out why. We didn't want to worry you."

Wow, Delilah was good. She told Ava the truth without releasing the bomb.

"Right, okay. Who was the buyer?"

Not that good. Delilah and I gave each other a long hard stare before I said, "Nestle."

Ava's big brown eyes widened, "What?" She turned away, covering her mouth.

"I'm sorry," Delilah said.

"I don't know what to say. I can't believe you would sell anything to that man. I don't even feel like I can be mad about all this because it's my fault," Ava stroked her throat and grimaced.

"How is any of this your fault?" I demanded. "I'm sorry, I love your family, but what happened to them was not your doing. The fact that Nestle is some sort of crook preying on people is not your fault."

"I need to get out of here." She grabbed her purse, storming toward the door.

"Wait, where are you going?" Delilah begged for an answer.

"I'm going to find that man and deal with him."

"That's exactly why we didn't want to tell—"

Too late, Ava was out the door.

Delilah and I exhaled staring at one another in helplessness.

Bradley came bouncing down the steps, "I figured out your code!"

Chapter Sixteen

"*What if someone knows I'm the killer*?" I gasped staring from Delilah to Bradley.

"So, wait, Mod wrote that to Alyssa—not the other way around?" Delilah shook her head voicing her denial.

"How did you crack the code?" I asked Bradley.

"It's a common code. They used the alphabet backwards in the hopes no one was smart enough to know how to hack it," Bradley raised his chin.

"So, frail little Mod killed Darla—I can't—I just can't believe it." I stood staring at nothing, lightly shaking my head back and forth.

"It makes sense since we found the height difference. She did it to throw everyone off making it look like it was someone taller than Darla, not shorter," Delilah said.

"With those stilts, she was definitely tall enough to be the figure in the mask," said Bradley.

"And Alyssa knew," I said.

"Lahiri said they told each other everything.

They would all try to protect each other," Delilah said.

"So, one or both of those guys bullied or forced Mod to do it for some reason?"

My phone rang, "Hello?"

"Hey sweetie, it's me," Mick said.

My heart fluttered from hearing him address me as 'sweetie.'

"Hi, how's it going?" I said, not giving a cutesy name back. I wasn't used to this yet.

"I wanted to give you a heads up that we had to release Quinn this morning."

"So, both Tad and Quinn are out?" I looked at Delilah.

"Gotta go, love you," I hung up and my eyes felt like they bulged out of my head.

Delilah and Bradley were both giving a wry grin.

"I can't believe I said that. He called me 'sweetie.' Oh no, he's going to freak out! I ruined everything!" I panicked.

"OR, he is standing there in shock, with a big smile on his face, thinking 'Finally,'" Delilah said nudging her brother's arm.

"Yep, I agree with Delilah—she's normally right."

"Smart man," Delilah and I said in unison.

"We need to get to the B&B and check on the girls if both of those guys are out of jail," I said changing the subject. I checked the camera feed on my phone. None of the girls were in the room. Maybe they had gone out for a walk or some food.

"You're right," Delilah said grabbing her

colorful canvas cross-over bag. "Ready."

"I have to work on a story, but I can put it off if you need me to go with you," Bradley said.

"Nope, we got this," I said.

Pulling into the drive of Make Yourself at Home Bed and Breakfast, I looked next door, to where Mick's Italian restaurant M&M's stood. The B&B was gorgeous, and being on the southeastern side of the village, it was located in a prime spot near the freeway, and they did great business.

It was a huge building that looked like an updated castle painted pale yellow with bright white shutters around the windows. There were symmetrical wings with towers at the top of each wing that had balconies on each tower with matching white railings for the balconies.

We paused in the car to discuss how to approach what we did next.

"Is it time to let them know who you are?" I asked Delilah.

"Yep, I don't plan to go back to that commune at this point."

"So, should we go and attempt to have an honest conversation with them?"

"We can try."

I noticed the beautiful, budding garden as we walked the cobble path to the entrance. Lahiri and Allison were huddled in a corner of the lobby, hunched together in conversation. There was a partitioned wall right next to where they were talking, so I nodded their way and casually crossed the beautiful maroon-and-light-grey marbled floor of the lobby. When we reached the partition, I pulled Delilah behind it with me. From here, we might be able to hear what they were saying.

Delilah was standing behind me, and I leaned around to listen.

"What are they saying?"

"Something about the mask—Allison says Poppy can't find it and that's why she came over here today—I think, now Lahiri is asking Allison why they didn't destroy it. Wow, so they were all in on it. You ready to go—Delilah?"

I heard a noise and turned to see Delilah lying on the ground. I looked up. "Tad?"

Then everything went black.

I was mumbling something and feeling drowsy. I think I was moving my hands, but I couldn't see straight. I was freezing; every limb in my body felt numb.

"Delilah?" I called out, slowly moving my head. I tried to stand, only to fall back over.

A voice came out of nowhere, "I see you are finally awake."

My head perked up and my skin prickled all over.

"Where are you?" Was I blinded somehow?

"Somewhere you can't see me."

"Your voice is weird. Why am I so cold?"

"You're in a freezer."

That's why I was so clammy, and it was dark with an odd stench. "I know you're not the killer. I know Mod killed Darla—I just don't know who killed Mod."

"How do you know Mod killed Darla?"

"We figured out the code."

"'Art is a lie that makes us figure out the truth'."

"So, you are Picasso's Peril? He said that before, in class. Is that you, Tad?" I groggily recalled thinking I saw Tad standing over Delilah when everything went black.

"It's an actual quote from THE Picasso. There's truth in it. Some only see the world as ugly—like being trapped in a freezer when you are bad. Other people like to beautify it." He seemed to ignore my question.

"You know people will be looking for me. What did you do with Delilah?"

Silence from outside of my frigid prison.

The wind was in my hair and Darla was driving the convertible with the top down.

"Why did Mod kill you?" I asked.

"She didn't have a choice. None of us had many choices." Darla's long dark hair flew in the wind as she gassed the car. It roared to life and jerked my body back—it felt like my body was shaking hard. The speedometer sped up to over one hundred miles an hour. She looked at me and smiled then her face took on a resemblance to the upside-down mask. Mod stood in the road up ahead—one moment she was short—the next she was tall wearing stilts like a clown.

I heard the voice again and felt myself cry out "NO!" I pushed hard as the voice grabbed me.

"Sweetie, Jolie—it's me. Can you hear me?"

"Mick?" I squinted. Everything was too bright.

"You passed out. You are freezing. We pulled you out of the freezer and you're in the car with the heater on now. Ava and Bradley are here."

"Delilah," I breathed out.

"She's okay. She's getting checked out at the hospital. Someone hit her on the head pretty hard. Last I heard she may have a mild concussion, but she said you had your laptop with you when the two of you went to the B&B. Tabitha put a GPS device locator on your laptop, so Bradley and Tabitha used it to find you."

"Why didn't Picasso's Peril steal it?" I mumbled, my lips and jaw still too stiff from the cold to speak clearly.

"What's that, baby?" Meiser asked. "Why didn't they take the laptop?"

"It's that huge tote bag of yours that you carry everywhere," Ava said. "No one else is crazy enough to go through it. They just tossed it in the bushes, which was their mistake! That's how we found you. Your phone must have been in your pocket, because it's gone. I guess I'll have to stop teasing you about carrying a suitcase with you everywhere."

"Where are we?" I asked, finally able to begin to make out shapes. Outside the window I saw a wooded area and an old abandoned cabin with a run-down building out back.

"Outside of Tri-City and Leavensport, deep in the woods, with not much around. How these two were able to track a signal, I have no clue," Meiser said. "We don't know whose place this is, but we will dig into it. That building out back is the freezer where you were locked up."

Chapter Seventeen

Mick drove me home while Ava and Bradley went to get my car from the B&B. I took a long, hot shower and put on a sweat suit even though it was a balmy eighty degrees outside, still trying to shake off the chill from the freezer. Summer was definitely upon us.

I walked downstairs to the kitchen to find my kitchen was full of people! Ava, Bradley, Mick, Tabitha, Teddy, Keith, and members of my family all scrunched together, and Delilah sat at the table.

I gasped and hurried over to her. "Delilah! I'm so glad you are safe. Are you okay?"

She stood and we embraced each other. "Me, I just got a knock on the noggin—you were the one who was chloroformed and taken off and locked in a freezer for hours. How are you?"

"I'm fine," I said as my mom, grandma, Aunt Fern, Uncle Eddie, and Uncle Wiley started scooching past people to get to me. "I promise guys, I'm fine. A lot has happened. I need to talk to these guys to find out what's going on. I'll come visit you all tomorrow—we'll have lunch or dinner together and I'll fill you in on everything."

"Promise?" Grandma Opal lightly touched my cheek.

I grabbed and kissed her hand, "Promise."

"Now that you two are an item, I am expecting a lot more out of you, young man. You will need to take good care of this one. I know I'm a lot shorter than you, but I'm not opposed to turning no young, strappingly handsome man over my knee if I need to," Grandma half-scolded, half-flirted with Meiser.

"Yes, ma'am. Noted."

"Smart man," Ava, the women in my family, me, and Delilah all said in unison then looked at each other and laughed.

The Tucker family dispersed, and I reached out to grab Uncle Eddie to hug him, "I'm glad you came with them. I know they haven't been welcoming. We will all work it out in time," I whispered in his ear.

Uncle Eddie was shorter than me by a foot—he must have taken after my grandma. He was balding with dark hair over each of his ears that met around the back of his egg-shaped head. He had dark caring eyes that also had a gleam of orneriness that I'm sure he got naturally. He was stout and sported old jeans, an Ohio State Buckeye T-shirt, and tennis shoes. "I'm not worried about these fools. I'm happy you are okay."

"Okay, so fill me in," I looked at anyone who had information to share.

"Tabitha was able to get a hit on the voice from recordings from the classes and found out it was a combination of Tad and Quinn together. You were right—" Meiser grinned sheepishly at me, "they were in it together. It started with Quinn forming the group. He already knew Tad and used him to help lure them all in when Tad started dating Alyssa then began having an affair behind her back with Darla. They used Darla for money, even though Quinn's family is rich too."

"So, who killed Mod?"

"Quinn confessed to doing it," Teddy said, "and Tad conspired. We got a confession."

"We're going to let you get some rest," Mick said looking at everyone as a cue to head out. He reached down and softly kissed my lips then whispered in my ear, "I love you, too."

Everyone left but Ava.

"So, did you kill Nestle?" I asked.

"That was the plan, but Gemma couldn't reach you, so she called me to let me know she broke the code and what it said. I came back to the house to tell you, but everyone was gone. I tried to call you and Delilah, but couldn't reach either of you, so I called Bradley since he had been here. That's when he told me where you two bone-heads went and we got worried and called Mick."

"Thank goodness you did," I said hugging her. "Are you still angry with me and Delilah?"

"No, you know I can't stay angry—especially when you fools go and get hurt."

"Yes, that was our plan."

"I still want to find Nestle and give him an earful."

"I have a notebook where I've been looking into it. After I rest up, we'll look it over and take it on as a PI case."

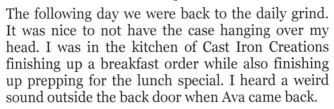

The following day we were back to the daily grind. It was nice to not have the case hanging over my head. I was in the kitchen of Cast Iron Creations finishing up a breakfast order while also finishing up prepping for the lunch special. I heard a weird sound outside the back door when Ava came back.

"Got their order done yet?"

"Yep, just plating it. Hey, do you hear that sound out in the alley?"

"Kind of," Ava went back to open the door that leads to the alley behind the restaurants where the dumpsters are and where we receive our deliveries. I took the bacon, sunny-side-up eggs, and toast to Magda to deliver to the customers.

"No way!" Ava crowed.

"What?" I said running to see what she was squealing at.

"Oh my God, I'm in love!" Ava was on all fours on the ground, reaching behind the dumpster.

"Don't sit there! Who knows what has fallen out of those dumpsters?"

Ava pulled out a tiny little black kitten that was mewing loudly. It must have been in the dumpster and that is what I heard because I saw a large can was laying in the alley.

"Oh my gosh, NO!" I cried. "So tiny and fluffy! We have to take it to Dr. Libby."

Ava reached back, "There's another one!" She pulled out a short-haired black, shiny kitten with a face the shape of a Siamese cat. It had the cutest little puckered-up stink face.

I took the fluffy one in my arms, while Ava held

the other. "Do you think there are more?"

"Here, give me that one too," I said, reaching for stink face.

Ava crawled over and looked behind the dumpsters, then looked inside the dumpster that had a lid open. "I hear something," she said.

"Hold on," I said, walking the babies around front and putting them inside my car. I cracked the window. Then I ran inside to let Magda know what was going on and that I'd be right back.

I went back to the alley and Ava was knee-deep in trash in the dumpster.

"I found one more," she said, handing out the chubbiest of the three. This black kitten had beans or something similar smushed on her face. "I dug through and couldn't find more."

"Well, I guess I'm going to officially be the crazy cat lady with curly hair at the young age of twenty-five," I said.

"Heck no, girlfriend! I found them. They're mine!"

"You want them?" I gasped. My best friend finally had cats of her own! I always dreamed this day would come.

"Yes, where are my other babies? I'm taking them in to Dr. Libby right now to see if she can tell the sex and figure out what we need to do next." Ava climbed out of the dumpster.

"Whoa, you are ripe!" I held the kitten in one hand and grabbed my nose and squeezed.

"Give it to me," she rolled her eyes.

"They are in my car." I thought she meant the kittens.

"Keys?"

"What—no way! You aren't driving my car smelling like that!"

"Come on, I need to make sure they are okay. I'll clean your car," she promised.

I couldn't resist giving in, watching Ava rock back and forth on her heels in excitement. I handed the keys over.

A few hours later, I was finishing up the lunch rush when Ava came in smelling much better and in new clothes.

"Well, what did you find out?"

"They are three sisters. I named them Lily, Luna, and Lulu." She had the biggest grin on her face. It made me chuckle.

"And you're in love with them!"

"They are so adorable and sweet. Dr. Libby is cleaning them up and going to take care of everything. She says they are only five weeks old!"

"Oh wow, that's so young. They are very lucky to have—"

I was interrupted when Alyssa walked into the restaurant. Ava and I both froze in our spot, feeling awkward.

"Hello, ladies. I wanted to pop in and thank you both so much for figuring out what happened. It looks like Tad and Quinn are going to be in jail where they belong."

"Why aren't you there too?" Ava asked.

"I didn't kill anyone," Alyssa was wide-eyed. She reached up and fiddled with the comb in her hair.

"No, but you knew Mod killed Darla and you didn't report it," I said, crossing my arms.

"As my lawyer told the police, Tad and Quinn threatened all of us. We had good reason to fear them. I was trying to help her." She pulled at a scarf she had around her neck and grabbed the heavy sweater she was wearing to fan herself.

"Aren't you hot? It's over eighty degrees outside today," I said.

"I hate being cold. As soon as I finish college, I'm heading to Las Vegas where it's triple digits."

"Why?" I asked.

"Past demons." Alyssa turned and waved as she headed for the door.

"Why does her entire outfit look familiar?" Ava asked.

"I know—that hair comb, scarf, jeans, the Kanji necklace and ring."

Alyssa stopped briefly to pet Spy who sat near Mirabelle at the exit. Spy growled at her, which was unusual.

We walked toward them as Alyssa walked out the door and around the corner.

"Did you see? She had a locket with a cast iron skillet on it hanging from her purse, just like you two have!" Mirabelle said excitedly.

"Oh no! Everything she was wearing ..." I said grabbing Ava's arm.

"... was something from each person in the commune," Ava said as we ran out after her.

She was gone.

Chapter Eighteen

Ava and I strode through the door of the police station. Our staff agreed to cover us for a few minutes so we could let the police know what had happened. Teddy and Keith looked up, startled. Meiser came out of a back office.

"What's up, ladies?" Teddy asked.

"Something's not right," I stuttered. "Alyssa stole my necklace! But not just that. She stole things from everyone." I realized I wasn't making sense.

"Do you want to fill out a police report on the stolen property? We can send a cruiser over to her address." Keith handed me a clipboard with a form on it.

"It's not that, it's something else." Ava shook her head. "There was something about the way she was acting. It was ... strange."

Meiser looked serious. "Tell me what happened." He sat down at a desk and offered us a chair.

"She came into the restaurant and said she was

leaving town when she graduated, said something about her past. But she was wearing a weird collection of accessories—jewelry and scarves that I swear I've seen before on other people." I sighed. "I know I'm not making any sense. I'm sorry."

"No, everything you have said so far on this case has been right." Meiser took my hand. "I am learning to trust your instinct. I'll go over there right away and try to recover your stolen property, and ask her a few questions. Then when I get back, I'll question Quinn and Tad again. See if there is anything more they can tell us about Alyssa."

"Okay, thank you!" I exclaimed.

"I meant to tell you," Meiser added, leaning back. "I got the test back on the samples of the substance found in the field and on those caps. I was right. Premium cold-pressed extra virgin olive oil, imported from a small village in Italy. The village my family is from, in fact. It is that region's primary export."

"Oh wow! Why was someone dumping expensive olive oil in a field?" I wondered. "Have you ever used that kind in your restaurant?"

"I have before. I use a few different kinds. But I have no idea why there would be olive oil in a field near a bunch of holes." Meiser shook his head. He promised to let me know once he had finished investigating the necklace situation. Meiser snuck a kiss on my cheek, then Ava and I hustled back to the restaurant.

Business was steady for the next few hours. I popped up front between orders to look at the dining room. Bea came through the front door and over to the counter.

"Bea, I love your new look!" I exclaimed,

referring to her lack of glasses. "What does Earl think?" I looked over Bea's shoulder to see Lydia pushing the door open and getting in line behind her.

"Thanks, Jolie," Mrs. Seevers simpered. "Earl loves it. He says I look ten years younger. Can't keep his hands off of me!" She giggled. "Speaking of, I heard you and Mick are an official item now, not just 'testing the waters.'" Ava cackled and I blushed. I really wished Lydia hadn't come in at that exact moment.

"Can I get you a table, Mrs. Seevers?" I asked, trying to deflect this line of questioning.

"Oh, no, dear, I was just popping by to say hello and congratulate you on solving that case. I'm so glad those awful boys are behind bars. Okay, I'm going to go get my hair done. Earl and I have a date tonight!" Bea breezed back out of the door.

Ava rushed away to check on her tables, leaving Lydia and I standing awkwardly across the counter from one another.

"Uh, how are you feeling?" I asked stiffly. I think that is what you are supposed to ask pregnant people.

"Like a whale," she sighed. "A tired whale."

I nodded and cleared my throat. "Well, you look great." *Wow, this was uncomfortable.*

"Listen, I'm sorry you heard Bea say—"

"Jolie I'm really sorry that—"

We spoke at the same time. We both stopped and laughed.

"You go," I said.

"I'm sorry I lied about sleeping with Meiser. I'm just in a weird place emotionally right now."

"It's okay, it all worked out." We both looked down. She was really trying. "Hey," I said, "I've got a batch of fried donuts coming up in a second. Can I get you some?"

Lydia's face broke into a grin. "Oh yes!"

I sat on my couch that afternoon after work, munching on some leftovers from the restaurant. I was waiting for that satisfied feeling I always got when a case was solved, but it wouldn't come. I felt like some element of all of this was still incomplete. Sammy Jr. climbed beside me, rubbing his head on my chin. "Hey, Juju Bean," I cooed, scratching his head.

As I was musing, my phone rang. Meiser!

"Hey, sweetie. First of all, Tabitha is going to be at your house in a few minutes to take all of the spyware off of your laptop for you."

"Oh! Okay! Thanks. Now, did you find anything out about Alyssa? Did you get my necklace back? What did she say?"

"Jolie, she's gone. Completely gone." *Gone? What on earth?* "It looks like she packed some clothes and her car is gone. I put out an APB with the description, but I'm not holding out a lot of hope."

"An APB? Are you going to arrest her for stealing my necklace?"

"No, there's more to it than that. After I went to the house, I came back and Teddy, Keith, and I questioned those guys again. As soon as they found out Alyssa was gone, they spilled everything."

"Wait, what? What did they say?"

"Well, first of all, that house she took you to, that was Alyssa's childhood home. Her parents lived there for a while after that but then they were homeless." I shivered at the memory of waking up trapped in the freezer. *Alyssa was homeless? Poor girl. That does something to a person.* "Tad said that she had to find ways to provide for her own parents."

"I can't imagine having a childhood like that," I whispered. Then something he said made me snap to attention, "Wait, Tad said—he wasn't the one who hit Delilah and took me?"

"Nope, he had an alibi for that—you were right, though—you saw Poppy dressed as Tad—she and Alyssa took you out the back exit to get you in the car they had waiting by the emergency exit. Also, part of the reason they did it is because I guess Poppy was in disguise at Cast Iron Creation as an elderly lady and overheard you all talking about Delilah being undercover. She told Alyssa all about it."

The woman with the walker!

"Tad was in love with her for a while, Quinn said, and would do anything she said. Then once he started seeing her for who she was, he was already in too deep. Alyssa was manipulating all of them. She found each person's pressure point and squeezed. Oh, and all of the jewelry and accessories you saw her wearing? She holds onto some item from each person she controls. Hair combs, scarves, rings. It sounds like she is a collector, keeping souvenirs from people she controls.

"Quinn acted like the leader, but she had him wrapped around her finger. It was her idea to have them all move in together. She told him he would have the power if he would listen to her. Tad said she would always say, 'Art was a lie to make things seem beautiful—but I don't mind living a lie. I spent a lifetime living a lie.'"

I shook my head. What a warped psychology.

"Lahiri told Alyssa her history with one of her old professors, so she was under Alyssa's thumb. Mod had been bullied as a kid and Alyssa convinced Darla to bully Mod again—then played Mod telling her she had to stand up for herself—lots of behind the scenes fights happening at that lovely little commune, apparently. She got Poppy to lie to Darla about getting her a job in Hollywood, just sowing the seeds of anger and discord."

"I can't believe she convinced Mod to murder Darla!" I exclaimed.

"Quinn said that Alyssa hated Darla. Alyssa had a really rough childhood, grew up poor, and Darla had the rich girl life she always wanted. She manipulated Darla and got her to set up with this big plan to embarrass Mod in your class. Then she turned around and told Mod what Darla was going to do. Fed her a bunch of ideas, like that Darla's family was rich enough they could hire someone to kill Mod, and maybe Alyssa too, for defending her. She got Mod so scared and angry, and then planted that cast-iron stake in her path."

"Wow. That is nauseating." I put my hand over my mouth.

"She brought Poppy and Lahiri in on it to figure out a hack so that it wouldn't look like Mod was away from her camera while she did the deed. Tabitha said with the computer learning management system you two used, it was easy to choose green screen backgrounds and take a snapshot and then freeze the screen. That's what they did when Mod went to kill Darla—and keep in mind, she didn't have to go far to do it, take the stilts off, and get back to her spot. Then she forced Quinn and Tad to follow Mod to campus and beat her up, her 'mugging,' and then poison her after that."

"She's a puppet master . . ." I said, shaking a little, "the killer who doesn't kill."

We took a moment to process everything that had happened.

"Is that enough material to charge her with a crime, once you find her?" I asked with revulsion.

"If we find her," Meiser replied. "From what I've gathered, she's been lying and manipulating people her whole life, she is really good at getting away with things. But we're looking."

"Okay, Mick," I sighed. "I'm going to fill Ava in on all of this. It looks like we didn't crack the case after all. The mastermind is still at large."

"Huh, you're right. Neither of us won." Meiser gave a sad, world-weary chuckle and hung up. Just then, there was a knock at the door. Tabitha!

"Come on in," I said.

"Want me to get all of that stuff off of your computer?" she asked, smiling.

"Please! Also, Ava is going to be over here in a minute, I hope that's okay."

"No trouble at all, I'm the one invading your space."

Twenty minutes later, Ava sat on my couch, with her mouth hung open. I had just repeated everything Meiser had told me. She shook her head.

"That whole situation is twisted." Ava threw her hands up. "It's like a Shakespearean tragedy!"

Tabitha had been sitting quietly, working on my laptop, but she had heard everything, of course. She cleared her throat. "If I may?" She looked back and forth between us.

"Yes, of course, what do you think of all of this?" I asked.

"It sounds like a lot of the people in this situation have a dark past, especially Alyssa." Tabitha's voice was calm and informative. "She grew up manipulating people to survive. She was probably very good at it. Those kinds of people tend to be able to read someone and know immediately how to control them. For example, Quinn comes from money, likes power, she gave him that and then was his puppet master.

"It is possible, though, that trauma from her childhood may have made her mentally ill. She may be delusional. You'd be shocked to see some of the things traumatized people do. They can seem balanced and healthy, and then ..."

That thought made me sad. Not only did people do awful things, they did awful things because they were hurting.

"Okay, here you go," Tabitha scooted my laptop back to me. "It's clean." She picked up her bag and headed for the door. She turned one last time. "You did good work, Jolie."

I grinned. "Thanks." I knew she didn't just mean on the case.

I paused and tapped my pen against my chin, looking at the blank journal page in front of me. I needed to get my thoughts down.

June 2020

I'm twenty-five and I still have trust issues. I believed Alyssa. I really did. Being wrong about her has really shaken me. She took my skillet necklace, and she kind of earned it, because she was manipulating me just like she was manipulating all the others.

On the other hand, things are going really well with Meiser. We have gotten through a lot of our problems and are communicating really well. He listens to me and takes me seriously, which is what I need in a relationship. Of course, there are still some things that I don't know about him, but no relationship is perfect.

Tom Costello proposed to my grandma! It is so exciting. She is keeping him on his toes by saying she needs to think about it. I bet she'll say yes. Those two are really good together.

Aunt Fern and Mayor Nalini are still an item, and it seems to be going well.

Speaking of love, I helped Ava go shopping for an engagement ring the other day. She's going to pop the question! I'm so excited I can't stand it.

Everyone who lived at the commune was charged with crimes, but they got very light sentences because they were all considered to be under duress. I heard that Lahiri is related to Mayor Nalini somehow, which explains why the women didn't even end up having to serve any time. I heard they got time served with therapy and community service. I'm still trying to decide how I feel about all of that.

I can't stop wondering where Alyssa went, and if she'll ever come back. She did so many terrible things right under our noses and we didn't realize it until it was way too late. It makes me *wonder if she did decide to come back, if anyone would even see her coming.*

Recipes

Below are the NINE recipes that Jolie and Ava would have LOVED to get through with their "Cooking with Cast Iron" class—luckily, they can still share the recipes with all of you!

Potato Soup

Recipe taken and slightly altered from: https://afarmgirlskitchen.com/loaded-baked-potato-soup/

Prep Time: 15 mins

Cook Time: 15 mins

Total Time: 30 mins

Creamy and delicious Loaded Baked Potato Soup is easy to make in your Dutch oven cast iron pot.

Ingredients

- 7-8 baking potatoes peeled, cut into 1/2-inch cubes
- 2 medium onions chopped
- 3 cloves garlic minced
- 4 tablespoons butter
- 1/2 cup all-purpose flour
- 6 cups chicken broth
- 2 cups half and half
- salt and ground pepper to taste
- 1 teaspoon ground mustard
- 1/2 teaspoon onion powder
- 1/4 teaspoon garlic powder

- 1 pound bacon cooked crispy, crumbled
- shredded cheese, variety of your choice
- full-fat sour cream
- green onion thinly sliced

Instructions

In a cast iron Dutch oven:

1.   Brown the bacon in a Dutch oven pot over medium to high heat. Remove from the pan using a slotted spoon. Set on a few paper towels to drain the fat.

2.   Drain all but 1 tablespoon or so of the bacon fat. Saute the onions and garlic in the fat, just until translucent. Stir occasionally with a wooden spoon. Add the butter and let melt. Add the flour and cook for 1-2 minutes, or until it's lightly browned. Stir with a wooden spoon so it does not stick to the pan.

3.   Add the chicken stock and potatoes. Bring to a boil, then reduce to a simmer. Simmer the potatoes for 20-30 minutes, or until tender. Mash with a potato masher. Season with salt and ground pepper to taste.

4.   Gently stir in the half and half, a little at a time. Season with onion powder, garlic powder, and ground mustard. Add more ground pepper if necessary. Stir with a spoon occasionally. Let simmer over medium to low heat for 10-15 minutes, or until the soup is thickened slightly.

5.   Serve with a dollop of sour cream, green onion, shredded cheese and crumbled bacon, or a garnish of shredded, potatoes, fried pressed together in a cookie cutter.

6.   Enjoy!

Cast Iron Skillet Steak

***This is a Jolie Tucker—straight from Cast Iron Creation's kitchen—giving you two alternatives for making your steak!

Ingredients

- Coarse salt, such as kosher salt or sea salt
- 1 or 2 boneless beef steaks, 1 inch thick (about 2 pounds total), such as strip, rib-eye, flat iron, chuck-eye, hanger or skirt (preferably "outside" skirt)
- Black pepper (optional)

(Optional) I like to make my own rub for meat by combining paprika, garlic powder, cayenne, onion powder, and chili powder. Once the steak thaws, I put it in a freeze lock bag and add a dash of lime juice and rub to it to create a paste and rub it into the meat. I add real crushed garlic in and a splash of sriracha sauce, Worchester sauce, and a little more lime juice and let it marinade 48 hours.

Instructions

1. Remove packaging and pat meat dry with paper towels—see directions about for rub and marinade if you'd like to have more tender and flavorful steak. Line a plate with paper towels, place meat on top and set aside to dry further and come to cool room temperature (30 to 60 minutes, depending on the weather). Turn occasionally; replace paper towels as needed.

2. Place a heavy skillet, cast-iron, on the stove and sprinkle lightly but evenly with about 1/4 to 1/2 teaspoon salt. Turn heat to high under pan. Pat both sides of steak dry again.

3. When pan is smoking hot, 5 to 8 minutes,

pat steak dry again and place in pan. (If using two steaks, cook in two batches.) Don't forget to use a dishtowel or rubber handles for a cast iron skillet.

4. Let steak sizzle for 1 minute, then use tongs to flip it over, moving raw side of steak around in pan so both sides are salted. Press down gently to ensure even contact between steak and pan. Keep cooking over very high heat, flipping steak every 30 seconds. After it's been turned a few times, sprinkle in two pinches salt. If using pepper, add it now.

5. When steak has contracted in size and developed a dark-brown crust, about 4 minutes total, check for doneness. To the touch, meat should feel softly springy but not squishy. If using an instant-read thermometer, insert into side of steak. For medium-rare meat, 120 to 125 degrees is ideal: Steak will continue cooking after being removed from heat.

6. Remove steak to a cutting board and tent lightly with foil. Let rest 5 minutes.

7. Serve in pieces or thickly slice on the diagonal, cutting away from your body and with the top edge of the knife leaning toward your body. If cooking skirt or hanger steak, make sure to slice across the grain of the meat.

8. Enjoy!

***Alternatives: a different approach to cooking a steak using cast iron is to add oil and salt to your cast iron skillet and sear each side of the steak for one minute on medium heat. Next, put the skillet in your oven to cook to your preferred temperature. When you take the skillet out of the oven, move the steak to another tray and add wine (I use a sweet red) in your hot skillet to deglaze and scrape with a spatula then add the steak back in the skillet and then use a spoon to baste the wine over each side of the steak—it makes your steak extremely moist!

Glazed Carrots

Recipe taken and slightly altered from: https://www.allrecipes.com/recipe/229669/glazed -carrots/

Ingredients

- 2 pounds carrots, peeled and cut into sticks
- ¼ cup of butter
- ¼ cup packed brown sugar
- ¼ teaspoon salt
- 1/8 teaspoon ground white pepper

Instructions

1. Place carrots into large cast-iron skillet, pour in enough water to reach depth of 1 inch, and bring to a boil. Reduce heat to low, cover, and simmer carrots until tender, 8 to 10 minutes. Drain and transfer to a bowl.

2. Melt butter in the same cast iron sauce pan; stir brown sugar, salt, and white pepper into butter until brown sugar and salt have dissolved. Transfer carrots into brown sugar sauce; cook and stir until carrots are glazed with sauce, about 5 more minutes.

Baked Asparagus with Parmesan

Recipe taken and slightly altered from:

https://www.simplyrecipes.com/recipes/bake
d_asparagus_with_parmesan/

Ingredients

- 1 pound asparagus
- 2 tablespoons extra virgin olive oil
- 1/2 teaspoon salt, less or more
- 1/8 teaspoon black pepper, less or more taste
- 1/2 cup loosely packed (about 1.5 ounces or 40g) shredded or grated parmesan cheese, or to taste

Instructions

1.   Prep the asparagus: Preheat oven to 400°F (205°C). Break or cut off the woody ends of the asparagus spears. For an added touch, if you want you can use a vegetable peeler to peel the skins off the base of the asparagus spears for a more elegant presentation.

2.   Toss with olive oil, salt, pepper, Parm: Arrange the asparagus spears on a foil-lined cast iron baking sheet and coat with the olive oil. Sprinkle with salt, pepper and the Parmesan.

3.   Bake: Bake at 400°F until the cheese begins to brown, about 8-10 minutes.

Southwestern Rice Salad

Recipe taken and slightly altered from:
https://www.recipetineats.com/cowboy-rice-salad/

Ingredients

- 1 1/2 cups brown rice, uncooked
- 2 3/4 cups water
- *Dressing:*
- 1/3 cup lime juice, plus more to taste
- 1/2 cup olive oil
- 1 1/2 tbsp honey
- 1/2 tsp chipotle powder (sub with smoked paprika + cayenne pepper)
- 1/2 tsp cumin powder
- 1/2 tsp garlic powder (or 1 garlic clove, minced)
- 3/4 tsp salt
- Black Pepper
- *Salad:*
- 1 red capsicum/bell pepper, diced
- 1 green capsicum/bell pepper, diced
- 1 small red onion, chopped
- 1 x 400g (14oz) corn kernels, drained
- 1 x 400g (14oz) black beans, drained and rinsed
- 3 tomatoes, watery seeds removed then diced
- 1 cup coriander/cilantro leaves, roughly chopped
-

Instructions

1. Place brown rice and water into a medium cast iron sauce pan over medium-low high heat. Place lid on. When water starts simmering, turn down to low and simmer for 15 minutes until water has evaporated and rice is firm / tender cooked. Remove saucepan (lid on) from stove, stand for 10 minutes, fluff with fork. Cool to room temperature (transfer to large bowl and refrigerate to speed up process).

2. Place Dressing ingredients in a jar, shake. Taste test, adjust to your taste.

3. Place Salad ingredients and rice in a bowl. Drizzle with dressing. Toss, then serve. Fantastic served straight away and even the next day!

Betsy's Love at First Sight Triple Chocolate Crunch Cake

****This recipe is taken straight out of Chocolate Caper's kitchen and is Betsy's original recipe for Jolie's birthday cake.

Ingredients

- Chocolate Cake:
- 1 3/4 cup Flour
- 1 3/4 cup Sugar
- 3/4 cup Cocoa high quality
- 2 teaspoons Baking Soda
- 1 teaspoon Baking Powder
- 1 teaspoon Salt
- 1/2 cup Oil canola or coconut oil
- 2 Eggs
- 1 cup Buttermilk
- 1 1/2 teaspoons Vanilla
- 1 cup Hot Water

Chocolate Buttercream:

- 1 1/2 cups Butter softened
- 1 cup Cocoa (if you are a chocoholic like Jolie Tucker—you can increase the amount of cocoa—you'd want to increase the milk and powdered sugar slightly IF you increase the cocoa to keep it from getting too dry.)
- 5 cups Powdered Sugar
- 1/3 cup Cream Half n Half or Milk
- Toffee candy of your choice—smash it up

with a rolling pin

Instructions

1. Preheat oven to 350 degrees.

2. In a large bowl, stir together flour, sugar, cocoa, baking soda, baking powder, and salt. If you have a flour sifter, sift all dry ingredients.

3. In mixing bowl, beat oil, eggs, buttermilk, and vanilla for 1 minute. Add dry ingredients to wet ingredients and stir until combined. Pour in hot water and mix together. The batter will be liquidy but that's a good thing -- it will create a moist cake.

4. Spray two 9-inch cake pans (cast iron baking pans make cake very moist) with non-stick cooking spray. You can also use three 8-inch cake pans for this recipe. Pour batter evenly into each pan. Bake at 22-27 minutes. Place toothpick or cake tester in the center of the cake to check if it comes out clean.

5. Let cool before frosting.

To make Chocolate Buttercream:

1. In mixing bowl, cream together Butter, Cocoa, Powdered Sugar, and Cream until light and fluffy. You may want to add more cream or milk depending on consistency. Once the cake has cooled and has been removed from pans, frost each layer with frosting.

2. Top with chocolate shavings, chocolate chips, sprinkles, M & M's or whatever your heart desires.

3. At the end, fold in your toffee or chocolate covered toffee into your chocolate buttercream

Recipe Notes

*This recipe makes three 8-inch thin layers to two 9-inch thick layers. If you would like to make a

thick triple layer cake, 1 1/2 times the recipe and use three 9-inch cake pans.

You can sprinkle some toffee on the top of your cake too after spreading the buttercream. This is one baked good that gets even better the next day if covered.

Cast Iron Mexican Polenta Bowl

***This recipe was taken and slightly altered from https://www.purplecarrot.com/plant-based-recipes/mexican-polenta-bowl

Ingredients

- 1 cup dry polenta
- 1 jalapeño pepper
- 3 cloves garlic, peeled
- 1 avocado
- 1 can black beans
- 1 pint cherry tomatoes
- 1/2 cup green onions
- 1/2 cup fresh cilantro
- 1 lime
- 4 tablespoons nutritional yeast
- 1 teaspoon salt*
- 4 cups water*
- not included
- Tools
- small bowl
- medium bowl
- large pot
- whisk

Instructions

PREP: Rinse and dry all produce. Mince the garlic, chop the tomatoes, green onions, and cilantro. Slice the jalapeño in half lengthwise, remove the seeds and membrane, finely dice and set aside. Peel the avocado, remove the pit, cube and set aside. Drain and rinse the black beans. Cut the lime in half and juice into a small bowl.

1.   Add 4 cups of water to a large Dutch cast iron pot, over high heat and boil.

2.   While waiting for the water to boil, combine the polenta, nutritional yeast, salt, and garlic in a medium mixing bowl.

3.   Once the water is hot, slowly whisk in the polenta mixture. Continue to stir the mixture as the water comes to a boil. Once boiling, reduce the heat to low continuing to whisk the polenta until water is absorbed and it has thickened, about 3 to 5 minutes.

4.   Once cooked through, spoon the polenta into bowls. Top polenta with tomatoes, beans, green onions, cilantro and avocado. Add in as much jalapeño as desired based on your affinity for spice.

5.   Drizzle lime juice on top, serve warm and enjoy!

Spicy Skillet Peaches

***This recipe was taken from https://www.foodnetwork.com/recipes/hot-peaches-3367633

Ingredients

- 1 cup sugar
- 1 tablespoon cinnamon
- 5 peaches, quartered, with peel on
- 1 stick butter
- 1 cup Cinnamon Schnapps Liqueur
- Vanilla ice cream, for serving

Instructions

1. In a medium bowl, combine the sugar and cinnamon. Toss the peaches in the sugar mixture until generously coated. Leave them in the mixture.

2. In a large cast-iron skillet, melt the butter over medium-low heat. Add the peaches and fry on each side for 1 to 2 minutes, or until softened slightly. Pour the schnapps into the skillet and lightly stir the peaches around to absorb some of the flavor. Light the schnapps on fire. It should flame off quickly.

3. Remove from the heat. Place the peaches over ice cream and drizzle with the remaining sauce from the skillet. Serve immediately.

4. Use extreme caution when igniting alcohol. Remove the pan from the heat source before adding the alcohol. Pour the alcohol into the pan and carefully ignite with a match or click lighter. Return the pan to the heat and gently swirl to reduce the flames.

Cast Iron Breakfast Skillet

***This recipe was taken and slightly altered from https://www.hy-vee.com/recipes-ideas/recipes/cast-iron- breakfast-skillet

Ingredients

- 2 tbsp. extra virgin olive oil
- 1 ½ lbs. red potatoes, coarsely chopped
- 1 red bell pepper, seeded and chopped
- ½ c. yellow onion, chopped
- 2 clove(s) garlic, minced
- ½ tsp. kosher sea salt
- ¼ tsp. black pepper
- 4 oz. fully cooked Spanish chorizo, sliced
- 1 (4-oz) can mild diced green chilies
- 1 c. shredded Cheddar cheese (4 oz)
- 4 large pasteurized eggs
- Fresh cilantro, for garnish
- Tools
- 10-inch cast-iron skillet

Instructions

1. Preheat oven to 400°F.

2. Heat olive oil over medium heat in a 10-in. cast-iron skillet. Add potatoes, bell pepper, onion, garlic, salt and black pepper. Cook for 12 to 15 minutes or until potatoes are tender and golden brown, stirring occasionally. Add chorizo and chillies; stir until combined. Sprinkle cheese evenly over potato mixture.

3. Create four 2-in. indentations in the potato-chorizo mixture, using the back of a spoon. Crack one egg into each indentation, ensuring the

egg is in contact with the bottom of the skillet. Bake for 12 to 15 minutes or until egg whites are set and yolks begin to thicken. If desired, garnish with cilantro.

Exciting News!

***A percentage of all purchases of *Turkey Basted to Death, Blueberry Cobbler Blackmail, and Cast Iron Stake Through the Heart* will be donated to the following two organizations! Thank you for helping those that live with MS and homeless youth! For more information about those navigating life with MS, please visit The MS Society's page at https://www.nationalmssociety.org/ For more information about homeless teens, please visit True Colors United page at https://truecolorsunited.org/

Deep Dish Pizza Disaster Blurb

Welcome to Leavensport, OH, where DEATH takes a DELICIOUS turn!

"NO! He's not the father. You're all wrong! The father is ..."

Everyone at the festival stood with their mouths hanging open as Lydia, who went into labor on Labor Day, revealed the identity of the baby's father.

Autumn is beautiful in Leavensport, Ohio, with the colorful leaves and that crisp bit of coolness that dissipates the humid air that blankets the village each summer—but a dark cloud appears when a merchant from Tri-City is killed at the Leavensport Fall Festival.

Suburbanites clash with villagers, an MS flare-up puts Detective Meiser in a wheelchair, two couples announce their engagement, and someone is poisoned! This Labor Day weekend will do more than honor the laborers of Leavensport and Tri-City—it will pit them against one another to find a killer.

Read on for Sneak Peek of *Deep Dish Pizza Disaster* Coming September 4, 2020

Chapter One

Those hot stale summer months had turned into breezy, brisk autumn days. Our little village of Leavensport's annual Lively Lavish Labor Day Festival was coming up this weekend and I was working hard to prepare a cast iron feast to sell at Cast Iron Creations' booth. The festival brought in all of the locals as well as many Tri-City merchants setting up booths to promote their businesses.

This would be the first year I'd run the booth with Ava and my official boyfriend, Detective Mick Meiser. We had now been together nearly four months, and I'd never been happier. My grandma was engaged to Tom Costello, Leavensport local grocer, Ava had plans to propose to Delilah soon, and Aunt Fern and Mayor Nalini were still dating. Love was definitely in the air in Leavensport!

"Hey, can you spare a minute to help me up front? Magda had to run a quick errand and we just got a rush," Ava stuck her head back through the push-through kitchen doors.

"Sure thing, let me *pop* these cast iron *pop*overs in the oven and I'll *pop* right out," I waggled my eyebrows at her and grinned.

"LAME." Ava rolled her large chestnut brown eyes, but I saw the start of a smile form as she turned back to the dining area.

Strolling out front, my blue eyes widened at the packed tables before me, "What's going on? This is an odd time for a rush like this. I don't recognize a lot of these as regulars."

"Tri-City folk coming in to begin getting their booths set up for this weekend. I'd imagine Meiser's place is hopping, too. Chocolate Capers will probably get a lot of business later before they head back to the city," Ava said.

"Good point. I'll text Betsy and give her a heads up." I grabbed my phone and sent off a quick text to our friend, then grabbed an ordering pad and pen in one hand and coffee pot in the other and began moving around to get some orders going and cups filled.

Lydia waddled in with Magda following close behind her. "Whoa, sorry, I never would have run out if I would have known we would get slammed!" Magda grabbed the coffee pot and the pad from me and took over.

"Hey, Jolie." Lydia rubbed her pregnant belly and blew out a long breath.

"You need to sit down at the counter for a minute?" I asked. Lydia and I had a lifetime of being frenemies. The last few months have been the most pleasant we'd ever been to each other consistently.

"If I can fit," she laughed.

"You're due soon, yes?" I asked, filling up a cup of hot water and giving her a miniature cast-iron box with different tea flavors to choose from.

"Thanks, yeah, I'm past due. I'm so ready to have this child." She poked around for something decaffeinated.

"Hey, Ava, can you grab Lydia what she needs, please? I need to get back to the kitchen to check on the popovers and start working on all these orders," I said, smiling and waving to Lydia.

I had been scrambling to get to all the orders and had just finished sending out the last of the rush when Carlos, our assistant manager and other cook came in for the dinner shift.

"Yabba dabba doo, Jolie, you should have called me. I would have come in early to help you," Carlos said, pointing to his Flintstone's T-shirt. He learned English from American cartoons and loved to wear cartoon shirts daily.

"We didn't expect to get hit so hard. It just happened and I just kept cooking," I said, wiping sweat from my brow, then walking to the sink to splash some water on my face and wash my hands.

"Well, I'm here now to take over." Carlos began cleaning up.

"I can clean up, and I'm so sorry I didn't get more prep done for you for tonight. I started on the poblano stuffed peppers—there are a few trays of them in the fridge." I pointed to our huge, stainless-steel refrigerator.

"That's great! And it looks like it has cleared out out there. I should be fine. You go and relax." Carlos smiled at me.

I decided to take him up on that. I grabbed my large brown leather tote from the office and moved up front to see if Ava was ready to head home. We always walked, biked, or drove—depending on the weather—to work together. Today was a beautiful sunny day, but we needed to stop by Fred the Farmer's Market to pick up some local fruits and veggies for some dishes I was preparing for this weekend.

"All set?" I asked her, grabbing my keys.

Mirabelle, our hostess with the mostess, had just been dropped off by her mom, Mary, and she had Spy, her seeing-eye dog with her up front. Mirabelle was in her twenties, short, pleasantly plump, with the hugest and most beautiful smile and the best personality anyone could ever ask for. Everyone adored her and normally when it wasn't her shift to work, people asked where she was.

"Hey, girlfriend!" Ava said as approached the exit. She and Mirabelle did their fist bump explosion and Spy wiggled his tush as he sat near his best buddy.

"Hi, Ava!" Mirabelle squealed in glee.

"Hey, what am I? Chopped liver?" I asked, palms up.

Mirabelle giggled, "Hi, Jolie!"

Spy gave a quiet woof.

"Hi, sweet lady," I said, giving her a hug. "You know, everyone has been asking where you were today. We tell them you can't work open to close every day. You are one popular woman!"

Mirabelle's smile spread across her face. "Really?"

"Of course, everyone loves you WAY better than they do Jolie," Ava said.

I froze and glared at Ava. Mirabelle laughed.

Driving to the farmer's market, I decided to take the long way and drive past the Village Community Center, Leisure Library, and Book Addict Bookstore since I loved to see the displays they all did around festival time to promote their businesses. The library had large inflatable dancing men and women dressed as different workers for Labor Day weekend. I checked my rearview mirror and not seeing anyone behind me, I slowed to a crawl to carefully look at the display window of books.

"Why don't you just pull over and park and we can go in?" Ava asked.

"Oh, okay!" I said and we got out to look at the bookstore and library displays. The library had a lot of non-fiction books on the origin and spirit of Labor Day, while the bookstore's display held fictional books that tied into Labor Day with canvas vintage bunting American flags hanging behind the books.

"Are we going in?" Ava asked.

"No, just looking," I said as I saw my Aunt Fern and Grandma Opal approaching us from the community center. "Oh, crap! This is exactly why I didn't want to stop!" I snapped at Ava.

"Don't blame me because your family is nuts!" Ava snapped back.

"Yoo-hoo! Ladies—" my Aunt Fern waved us down as I tried to steer Ava toward the car.

"They see us! Stop pushing me!" Ava yelled.

"Girls, stop!" My Grandma Opal yelled in a curt voice.

We froze.

"Oh hey, didn't see you there. We need to head over to Fred the Farmer's Farm Market to pick up a few things," I said, smiling and waving as I led Ava, who was trying to turn and wave while being drug by her elbow to the car.

"Jolie Lynn Tucker!" Grandma exclaimed. "Who taught you those manners?"

"You, mom, Aunt Fern, and Uncle Wylie," I said, giving up and crossing my arms across my chest.

Grandma's eyes narrowed and she shook her

head.

"Whoa, Aunt Fern, is that a new necklace to match your earrings?" Ava reached out to touch the gold necklace.

"Yep, Fitan got it for me."

I still wasn't used to hearing anyone call the mayor by his first name and it freaked me out a bit. Mayor Nalini had courted my Aunt Fern as her secret admirer earlier at the beginning of the summer. That was when Ava and I tried our hand at culinary online cooking courses that turned out to be disastrous in more ways than one. One of our students, Lahiri, who had been a co-conspirator was now free and we found out she is related to Fitan Nalini. I still wondered if that is why she got off so easily. I tried talking to Aunt Fern about it before, but she would have *no trash talk about her man.*

"Very nice," I said. "Were you two working at the community center?"

"Yep, we were setting up the dining room and helping to get things set up in the kitchen as much as possible. We want people have the opportunity to eat and socialize inside if they so choose this weekend," Grandma said.

"What decorations are you using?" Ava asked.

By the look on both of their faces, that seemed to be a sore topic.

"You know they have that stupid pole on the stage for some reason—" Grandma started.

"It's a beam to help keep the roof from falling in," Aunt Fern declared.

"Whatever. It looks like a stripper pole to me."

Ava and I side-eyed each other nervously.

"Anyhoo, I thought it would be a kick to get a male blow-up doll and make him into a Magic Mike character for the stage. You know, put him on the pole," Grandma put her hands on her hips.

I stood frozen in my spot while my blue eyes darted around inside my sockets. I could see Ava's body trembling probably to contain a laugh.

"Right? Isn't that the most cockeyed idea you girls have ever heard in your life?" Aunt Fern shook her head. "I'm going to need to go see that therapist of yours with a mother trying to recreate strip scenes from movies!"

"I'm not touching that with a ten foot pole," I said as Ava could no longer hold it in and barked out a hearty laugh. The two of us jumped into my car and sped off toward the farmer's market.

"Seriously," I started as we pulled into the parking lot, "what is wrong with them?"

"Come on, they're funny!"

"Sometimes I'll admit to finding them a tad humorous, but man, can they ever give me a headache."

"Yeah, you did NOT get your sense of humor from them," Ava said as we moved toward the outside part of the market.

"You're not funny either," I said.

Ava bumped into my side, pushing me off balance. We grew up together and I was an only child, but Ava had a sister, Lolly. Ava and I were like siblings and best friends all in one. Our relationship was difficult for those who did not know us from birth to understand. There was a lot of loving bantering between us.

Fred the farmer stood outside under his red

and white striped awning near the bales of hay with pumpkins of every size sitting on around the hay. Colorful mums were displayed everywhere with boxes filled with squashes and zucchini and the like. Large bins of fresh-picked red and green apples were displayed on tables and nestled up next to them were large bowls of grapes and pears and buckets of cranberries.

"Well, if it isn't the two best lookin' ladies in the village! Who's the luckiest farmer ever to have you two grace me with your presence?" Fred stood beaming a large smile. He was a favorite of most people in the town. Fred Eddie stood about five foot five and always wore some sort of overalls or coveralls and work boots or rubber boots to match the weather and task. Today he sported his bibs with a green t-shirt underneath and brown leather work boots. His graying hair was full and pushed to the side, his square-jawed face had plenty of wrinkles typical of a man who had worn a smile most of his life.

"Hi, Mr. Fred the Farmer." Ava grinned. This is what she had called him since she was a kid.

"Hey, Fred! Your produce looks amazing as always!"

"You own this place?" asked a tall, lanky man with thick, black hair, a long narrow chin, and a mole under his nose.

"Sure do, sir, what can I do for you today?"

"I'm Ralph and own the pizza shop in Tri-City. I've heard great things about your produce. I figured while I was setting up my booth, I'd come here and buy the veggies for my pizza this weekend." Ralph enunciated each syllable of each word, making his sentences choppy and his tone seem demanding even though he seemed friendly enough by appearance.

"Whoa!" I exclaimed. "I'm Jolie Tucker and this is my friend Ava—we run Cast Iron Creations. We've had your New York style pizza and I have to tell you, it's incredible. Out of this world!"

"Well, thanks for the compliment dear. I'll pass it right back atcha. I just came from your shop for a bit of lunch. That skillet-fried chicken with cast-iron wilted bok choy seemed like an odd combo to me, but man, it packed a punch!"

"Thanks! I'm not pizza genius like you, but I love to make deep-dish pizzas in cast iron."

"Oh, yeah? Maybe I'll try that this weekend as another option inspired by you," Ralph said nodding his head as he moved toward the zucchini.

"Hey, beautiful," I heard Mick's voice behind me and felt tingles go up and down my spine. I turned toward him smiling. I turned and froze with worry as I saw him sitting in a wheelchair.

About the Authors

Moving into her second decade working in education, **Jodi Rath** has decided to begin a life of crime in her The Cast Iron Skillet Mystery Series. Her passion for both mysteries and education led her to combine the two to create her own business, called MYS ED, where she splits her time between working as an adjunct for Ohio teachers and creating mischief in her fictional writing. She currently resides in a small, cozy village in Ohio with her husband and her nine cats.

Rebecca Grubb utilizes her experience in the high school English classroom and her decades as a bookworm to coach writers and edit fiction and creative non-fiction. She enjoys reading and writing books, particularly mysteries and science fiction. She lives in a small town in Ohio with her husband and three mischievous children.

Other Works by Jodi Rath:

Book One: *Pineapple Upside Down Murder*

Short Story 1.5 "**Sweet Retreat**"

Book Two: *Jalapeño Cheddar Cornbread Murder*

Book 2.5 A Holiday Book *Turkey Basted to Death*

Book 3 *Blueberry Cobbler Blackmail*

Links So We Can Stay Connected

Be sure to sign up for a monthly newsletter to get MORE of the Leavensport gang with free flash fiction, short stories, two-minute mysteries, cast-iron recipes, tips, and more. Subscribe to our monthly newsletter for a FREE Mystery A Month at http://eepurl.com/dIfXdb

Follow me on Facebook at https://www.facebook.com/authorjodirath

@jodirath is where you can find me on Twitter

www.jodirath.com

Learn more about Rebecca Grubb's editing and writing coaching services at https://www.sterlingwords.com/

Upcoming Releases

Coming September 4, 2020, *Deep Dish Pizza Disaster*

Coming December 18, 2020, *Yuletide Cast of the Iron Skillet*

Coming April 16, 2021, *Monkey Bread Business*

Coming July 23, 2021, *Pork Chopped to Death*

Coming October 29, 2021, *Punkin Strudel Mayhem*